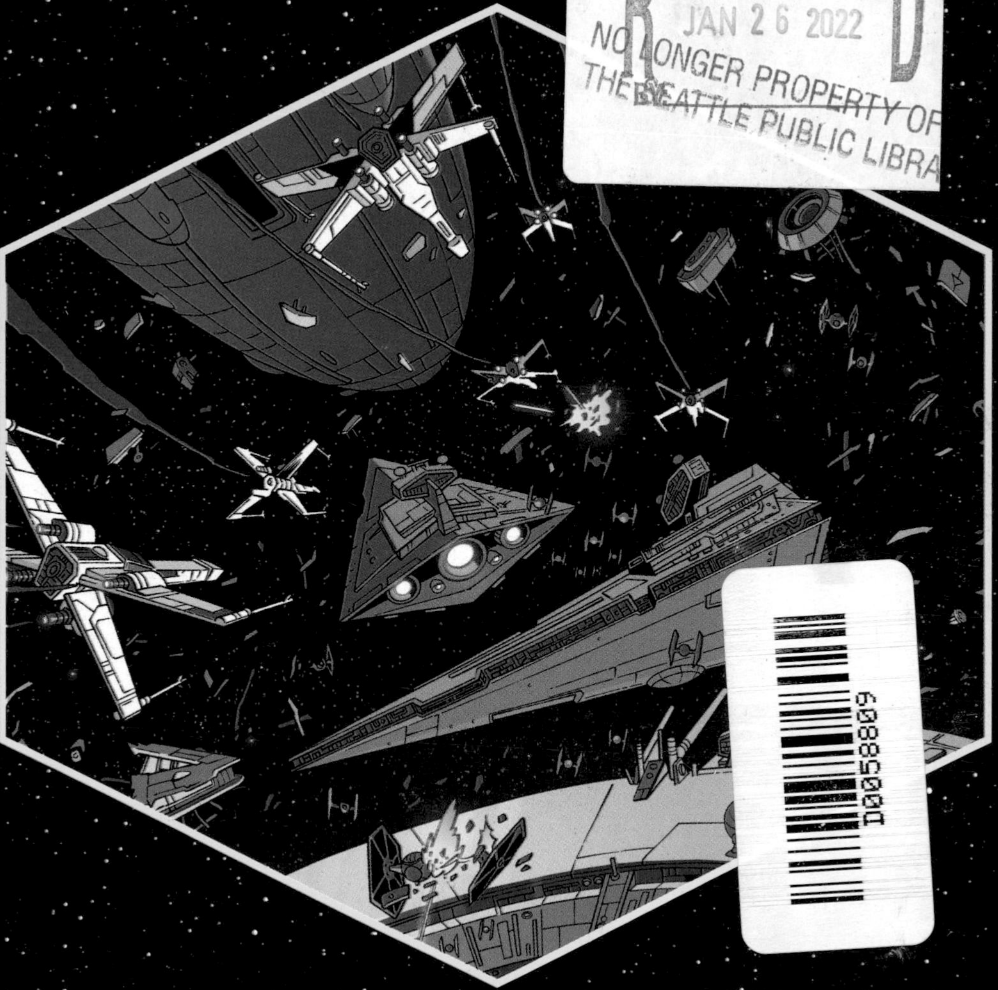

STAR WARS ADVENTURES

Destroyer Down

Facebook: **facebook.com/idwpublishing**
Twitter: **@idwpublishing**
YouTube: **youtube.com/idwpublishing**
Tumblr: **tumblr.idwpublishing.com**
Instagram: **instagram.com/idwpublishing**

ISBN: 978-1-68405-509-8   22 21 20 19   1 2 3 4

STAR WARS ADVENTURES: DESTROYER DOWN. JUNE 2019. FIRST PRINTING. © 2019 Lucasfilm Ltd. & ® or ™ where indicated. All Rights Reserved. © 2019 Idea and Design Works, LLC. The IDW logo is registered in the U.S. Patent and Trademark Office. IDW Publishing, a division of Idea and Design Works, LLC. Editorial offices: 2765 Truxtun Road, San Diego, CA 92106. Any similarities to persons living or dead are purely coincidental. With the exception of artwork used for review purposes, none of the contents of this publication may be reprinted without the permission of Idea and Design Works, LLC. Printed in Korea.
IDW Publishing does not read or accept unsolicited submissions of ideas, stories, or artwork.

Originally published as STAR WARS ADVENTURES: DESTROYER DOWN issues #1–3.

COVER ARTIST
DEREK CHARM

LETTERER
TOM B. LONG

SERIES ASSISTANT EDITORS
PETER ADRIAN BEHRAVESH
& ELIZABETH BREI

SERIES EDITORS
BOBBY CURNOW
& DENTON J. TIPTON

COLLECTION EDITORS
JUSTIN EISINGER
& ALONZO SIMON

COLLECTION DESIGNER
CLYDE GRAPA

Chris Ryall, President, Publisher, and CCO
John Barber, Editor-In-Chief
Robbie Robbins, EVP/Sr. Art Director
Cara Morrison, Chief Financial Officer
Matt Ruzicka, Chief Accounting Officer
David Hedgecock, Associate Publisher
Jerry Bennington, VP of New Product Development
Lorelei Bunjes, VP of Digital Services
Justin Eisinger, Editorial Director, Graphic Novels & Collections
Eric Moss, Senior Director, Licensing and Business Development

Ted Adams, IDW Founder

Lucasfilm Credits:
Senior Editors: Frank Parisi & Robert Simpson
Creative Director: Michael Siglain
Story Group: James Waugh, Leland Chee,
Pablo Hidalgo, Matt Martin

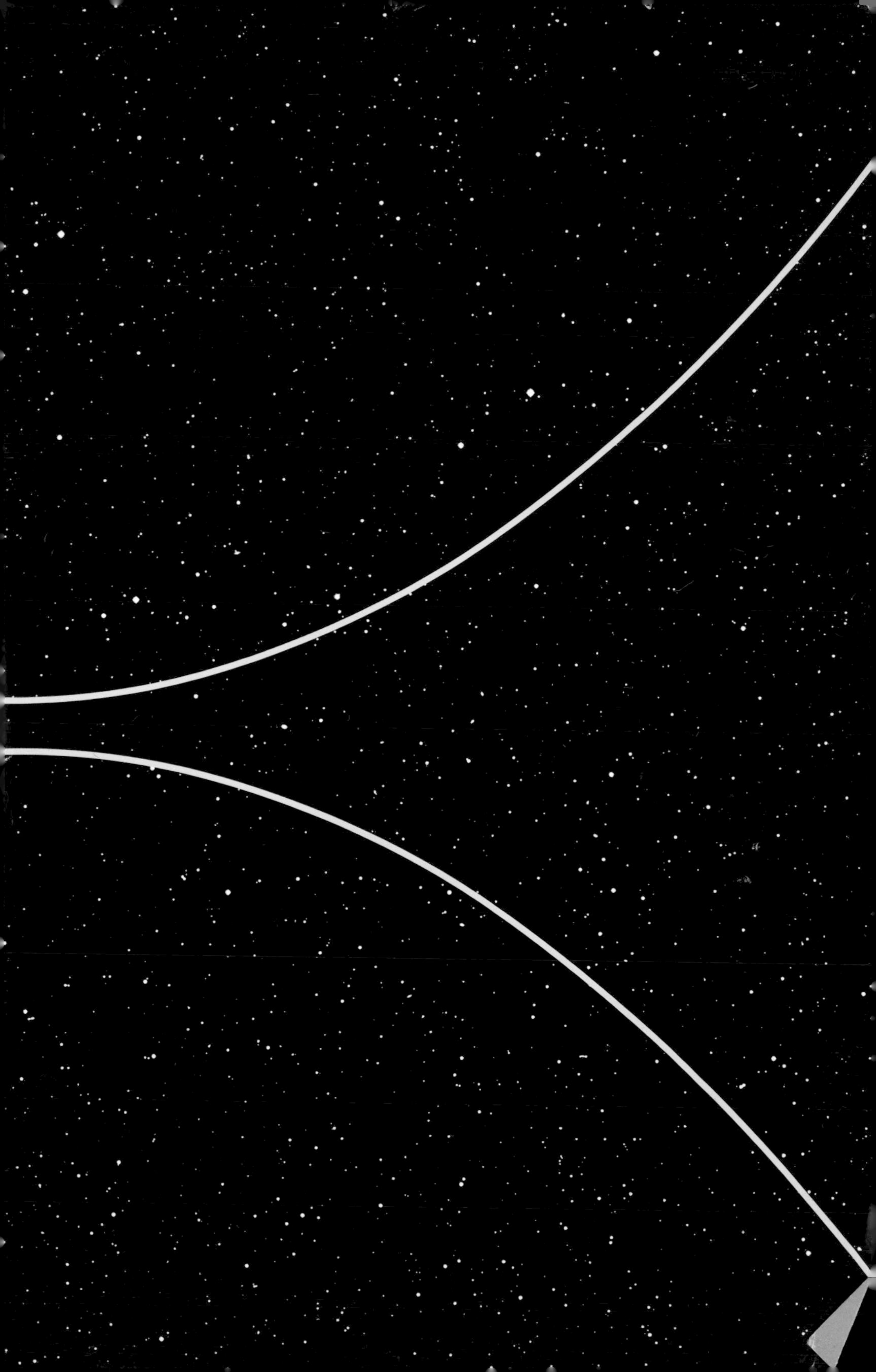

STAR WARS™ ADVENTURES

DESTROYER DOWN

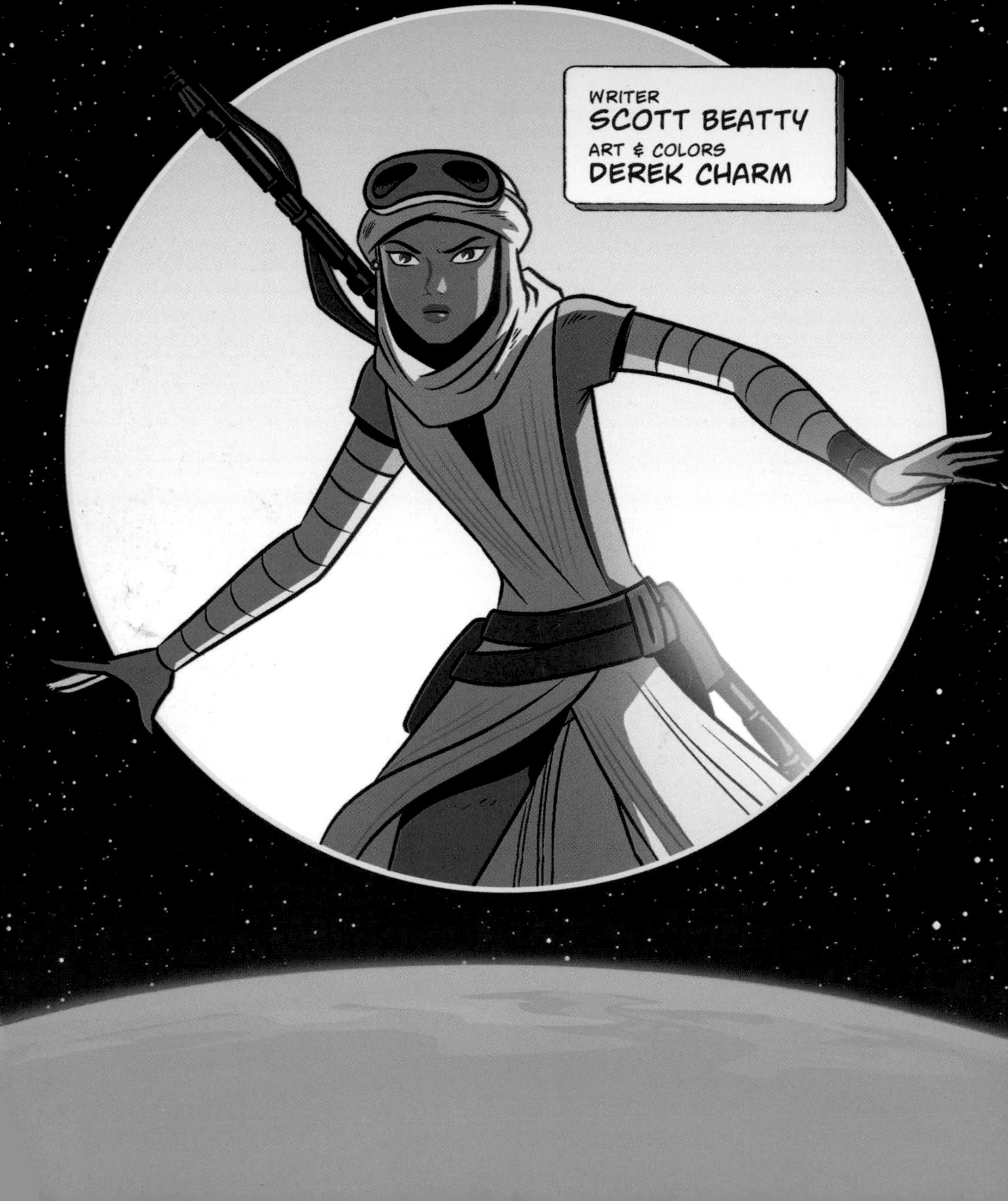
WRITER
SCOTT BEATTY
ART & COLORS
DEREK CHARM

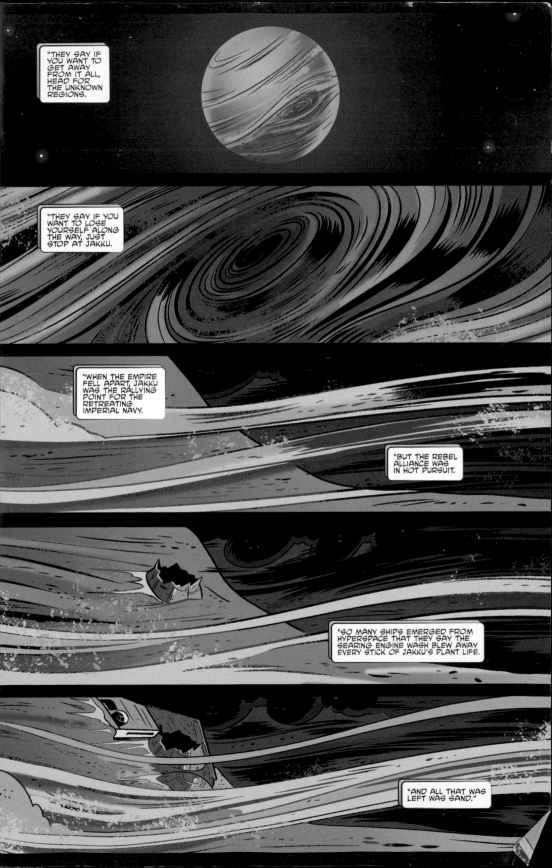

"THEY SAY IF YOU WANT TO GET AWAY FROM IT ALL, HEAD FOR THE UNKNOWN REGIONS.

"THEY SAY IF YOU WANT TO LOSE YOURSELF ALONG THE WAY, JUST STOP AT JAKKU.

"WHEN THE EMPIRE FELL APART, JAKKU WAS THE RALLYING POINT FOR THE RETREATING IMPERIAL NAVY.

"BUT THE REBEL ALLIANCE WAS IN HOT PURSUIT.

"SO MANY SHIPS EMERGED FROM HYPERSPACE THAT THEY SAY THE SEARING ENGINE WASH BLEW AWAY EVERY STICK OF JAKKU'S PLANT LIFE.

"AND ALL THAT WAS LEFT WAS SAND."

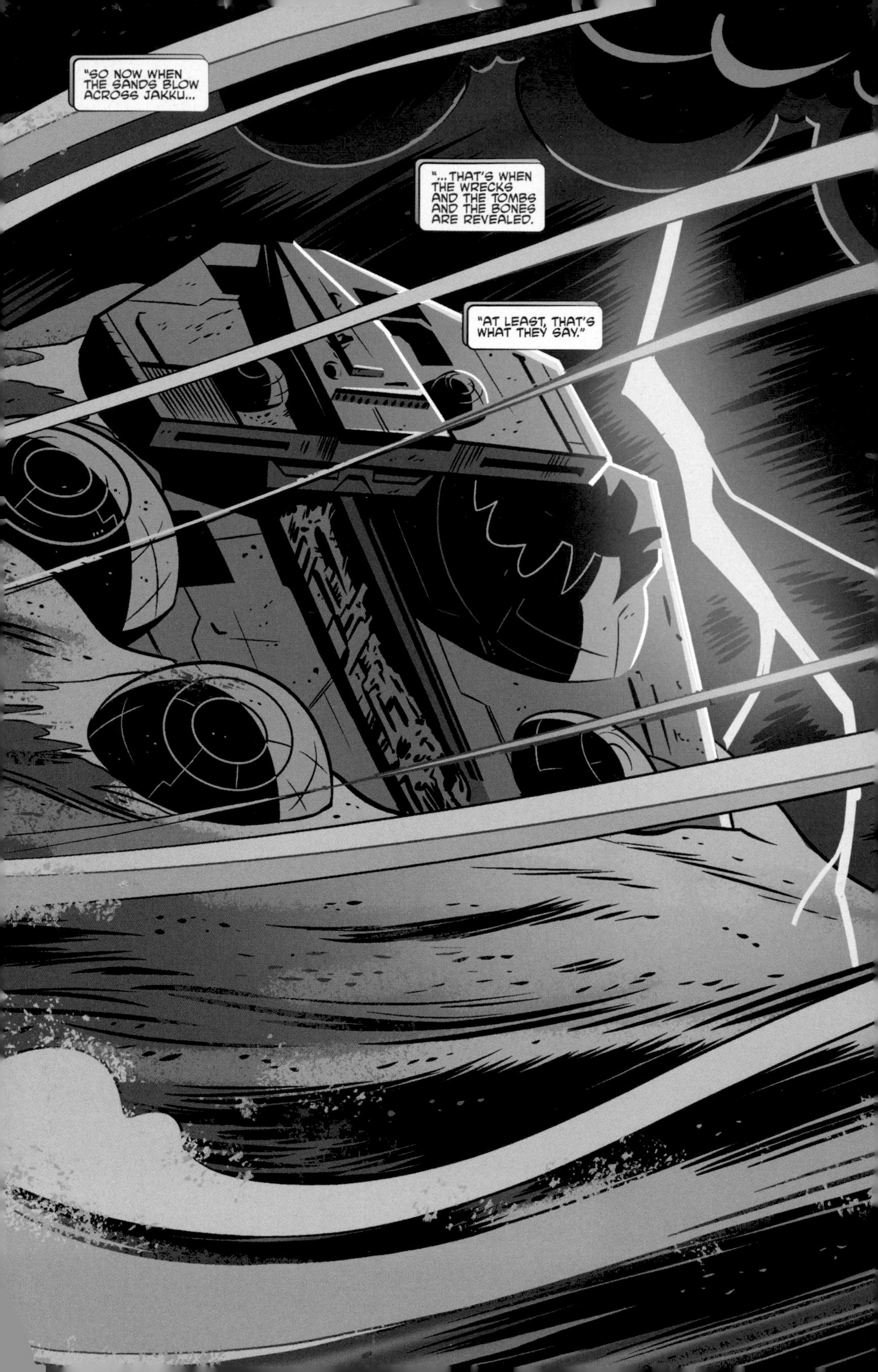
"SO NOW WHEN THE SANDS BLOW ACROSS JAKKU...
"...THAT'S WHEN THE WRECKS AND THE TOMBS AND THE BONES ARE REVEALED.
"AT LEAST, THAT'S WHAT THEY SAY."

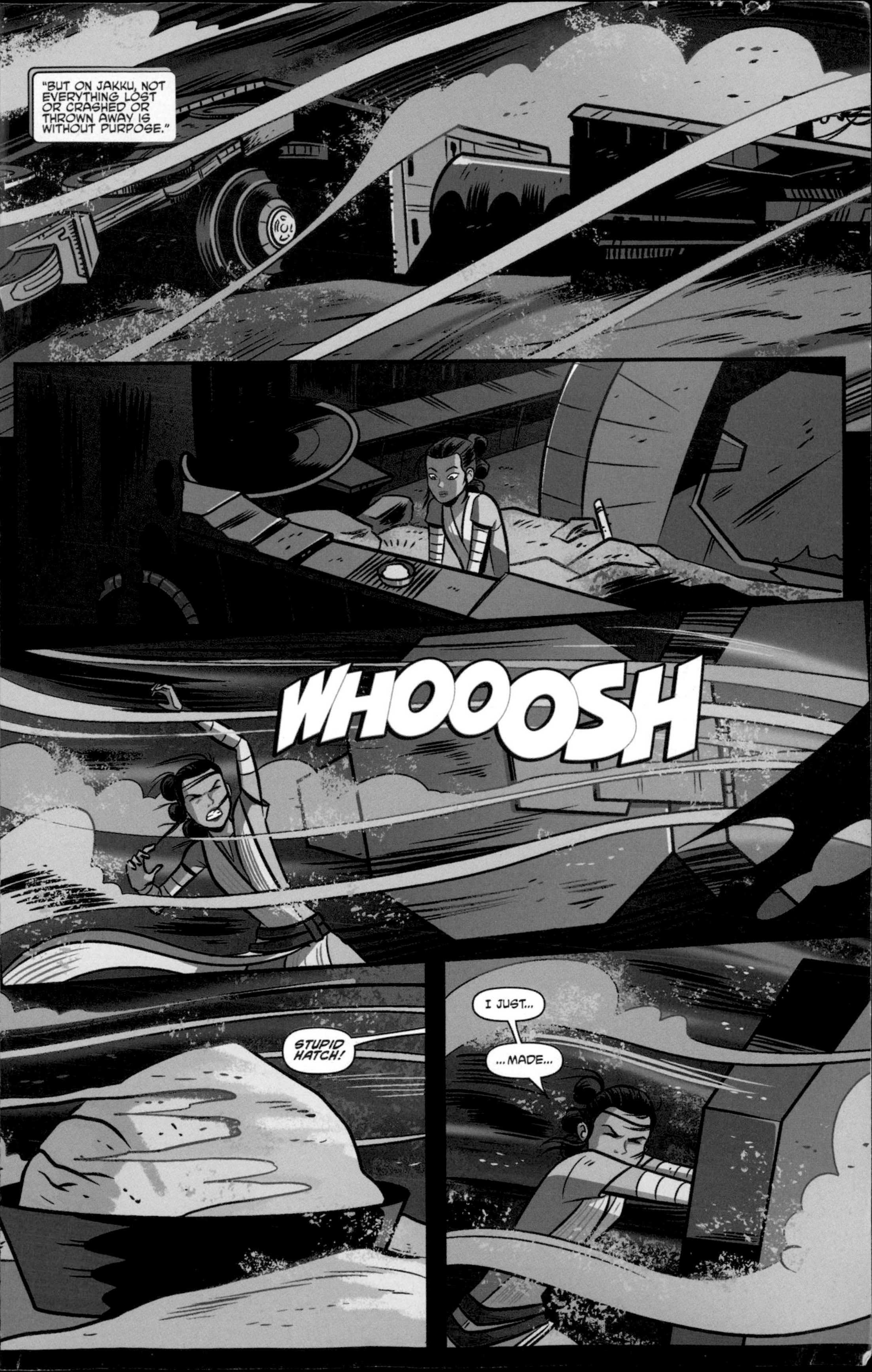
"BUT ON JAKKU, NOT EVERYTHING LOST OR CRASHED OR THROWN AWAY IS WITHOUT PURPOSE."
WHOOOSH
STUPID HATCH!
I JUST...
...MADE...

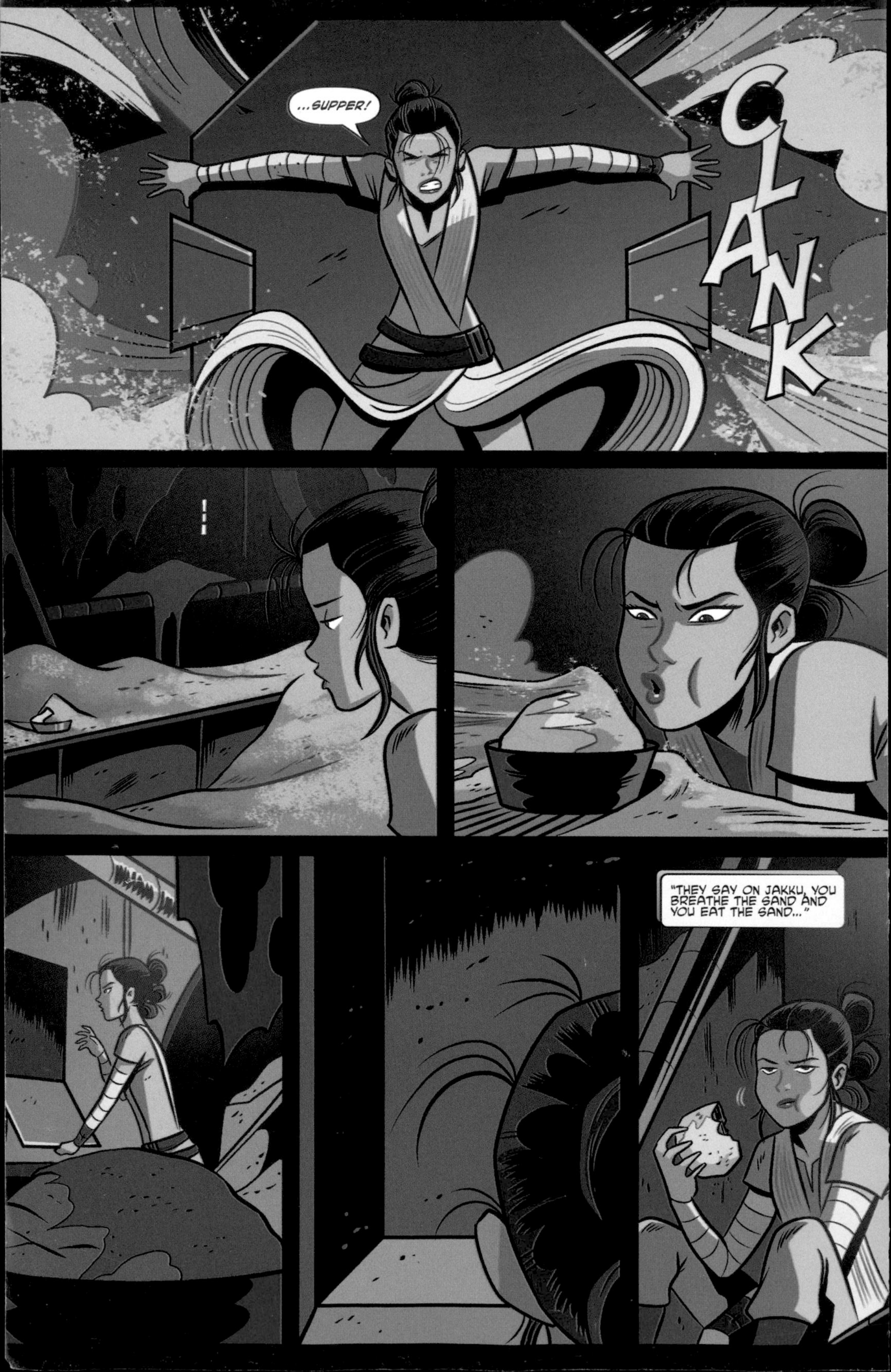

...SUPPER!
CLANK
!!!
"THEY SAY ON JAKKU, YOU BREATHE THE SAND AND YOU EAT THE SAND..."

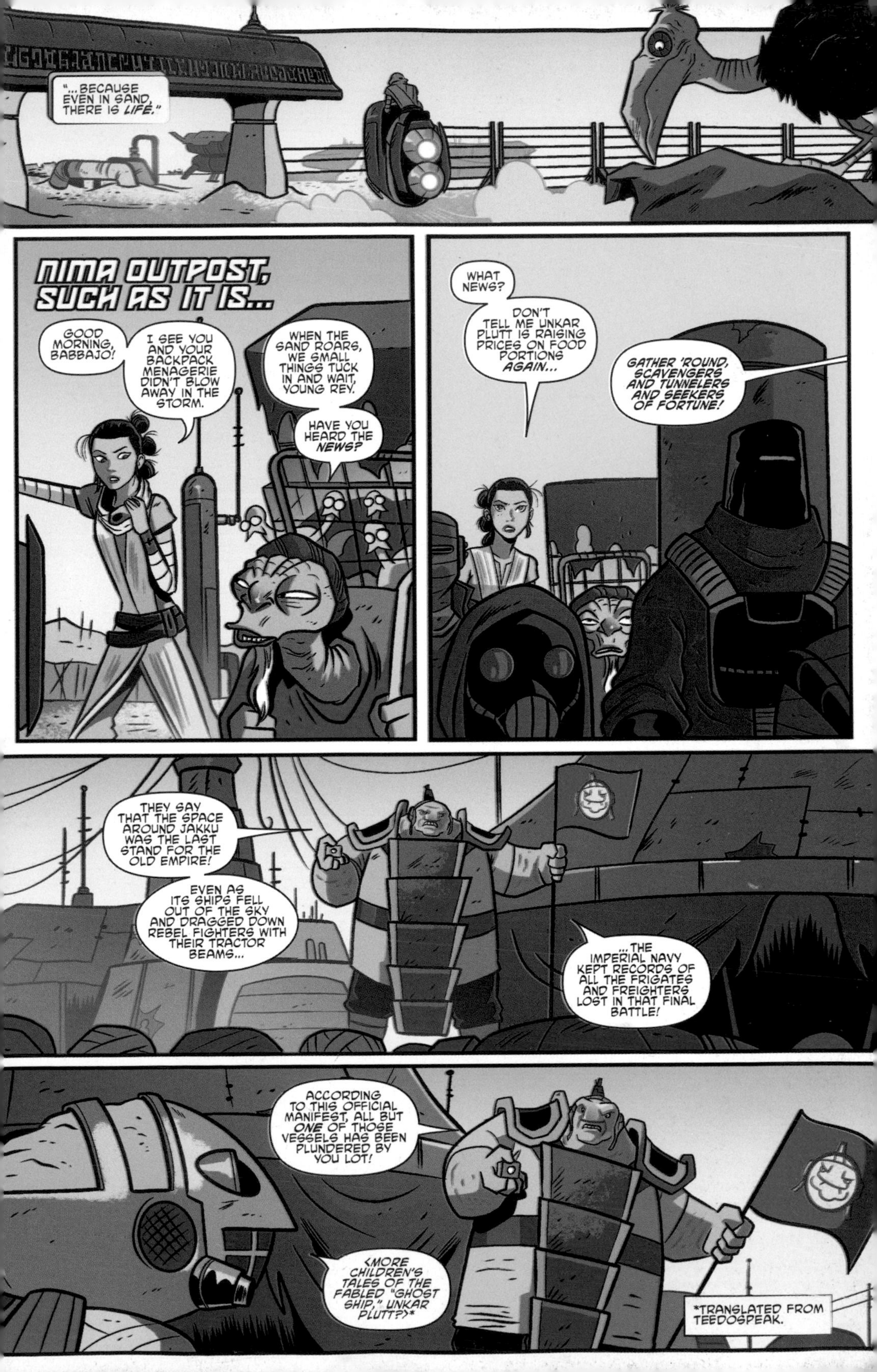
"...BECAUSE EVEN IN SAND, THERE IS *LIFE*."
NIMA OUTPOST, SUCH AS IT IS...
GOOD MORNING, BABBAJO!
I SEE YOU AND YOUR BACKPACK MENAGERIE DIDN'T BLOW AWAY IN THE STORM.
WHEN THE SAND ROARS, WE SMALL THINGS TUCK IN AND WAIT, YOUNG REY.
HAVE YOU HEARD THE *NEWS?*
WHAT NEWS?
DON'T TELL ME UNKAR PLUTT IS RAISING PRICES ON FOOD PORTIONS *AGAIN*...
GATHER 'ROUND, SCAVENGERS AND TUNNELERS AND SEEKERS OF FORTUNE!
THEY SAY THAT THE SPACE AROUND JAKKU WAS THE LAST STAND FOR THE OLD EMPIRE!
EVEN AS ITS SHIPS FELL OUT OF THE SKY AND DRAGGED DOWN REBEL FIGHTERS WITH THEIR TRACTOR BEAMS...
...THE IMPERIAL NAVY KEPT RECORDS OF ALL THE FRIGATES AND FREIGHTERS LOST IN THAT FINAL BATTLE!
ACCORDING TO THIS OFFICIAL MANIFEST, ALL BUT *ONE* OF THOSE VESSELS HAS BEEN PLUNDERED BY YOU LOT!
<MORE CHILDREN'S TALES OF THE FABLED "GHOST SHIP," UNKAR PLUTT?>*
*TRANSLATED FROM TEEDOSPEAK.

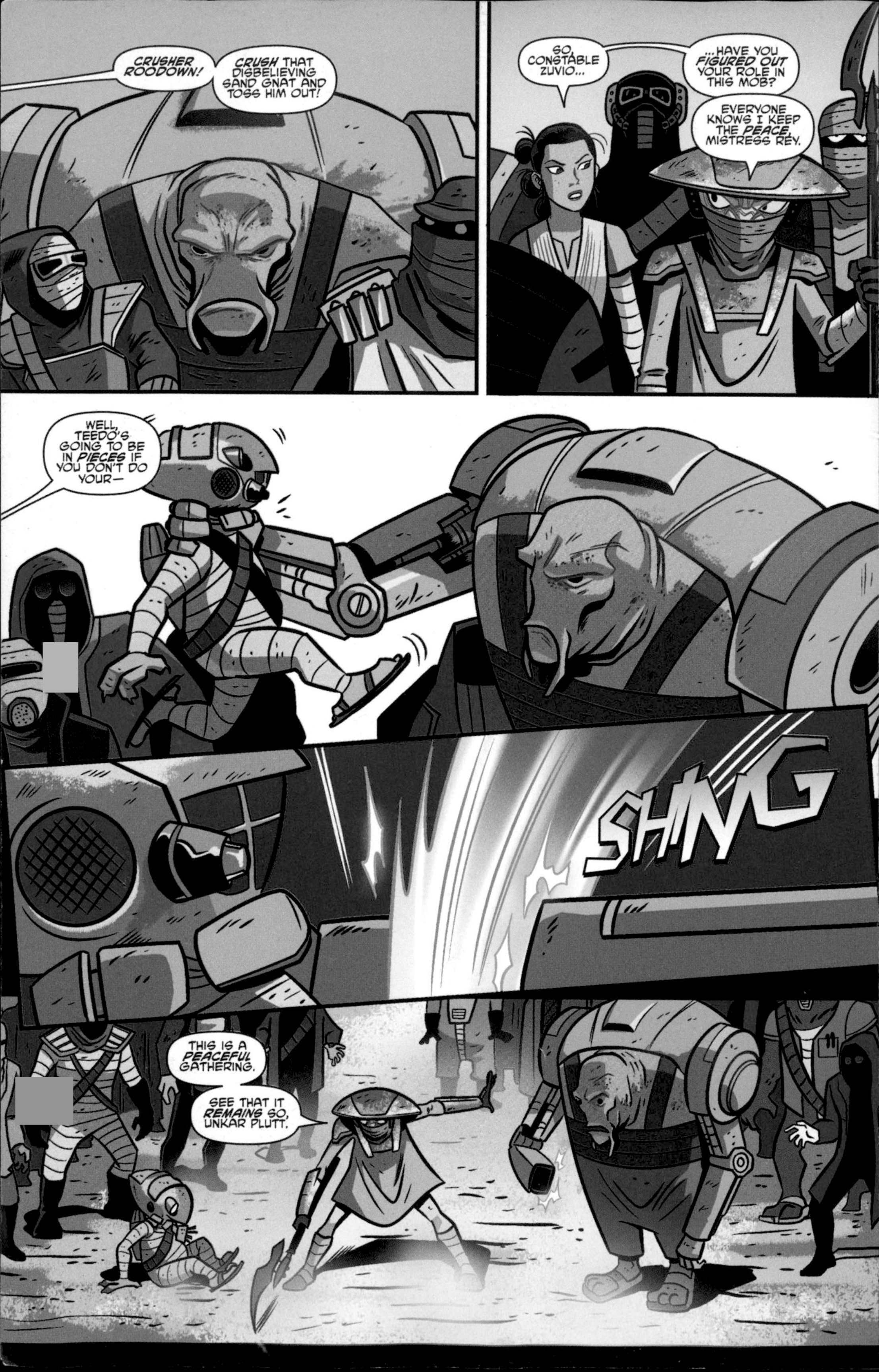

CRUSHER ROODOWN!
CRUSH THAT DISBELIEVING SAND GNAT AND TOSS HIM OUT!
SO, CONSTABLE ZUVIO...
...HAVE YOU FIGURED OUT YOUR ROLE IN THIS MOB?
EVERYONE KNOWS I KEEP THE PEACE, MISTRESS REY.
WELL, TEEDO'S GOING TO BE IN PIECES IF YOU DON'T DO YOUR—
SHING
THIS IS A PEACEFUL GATHERING.
SEE THAT IT REMAINS SO, UNKAR PLUTT.

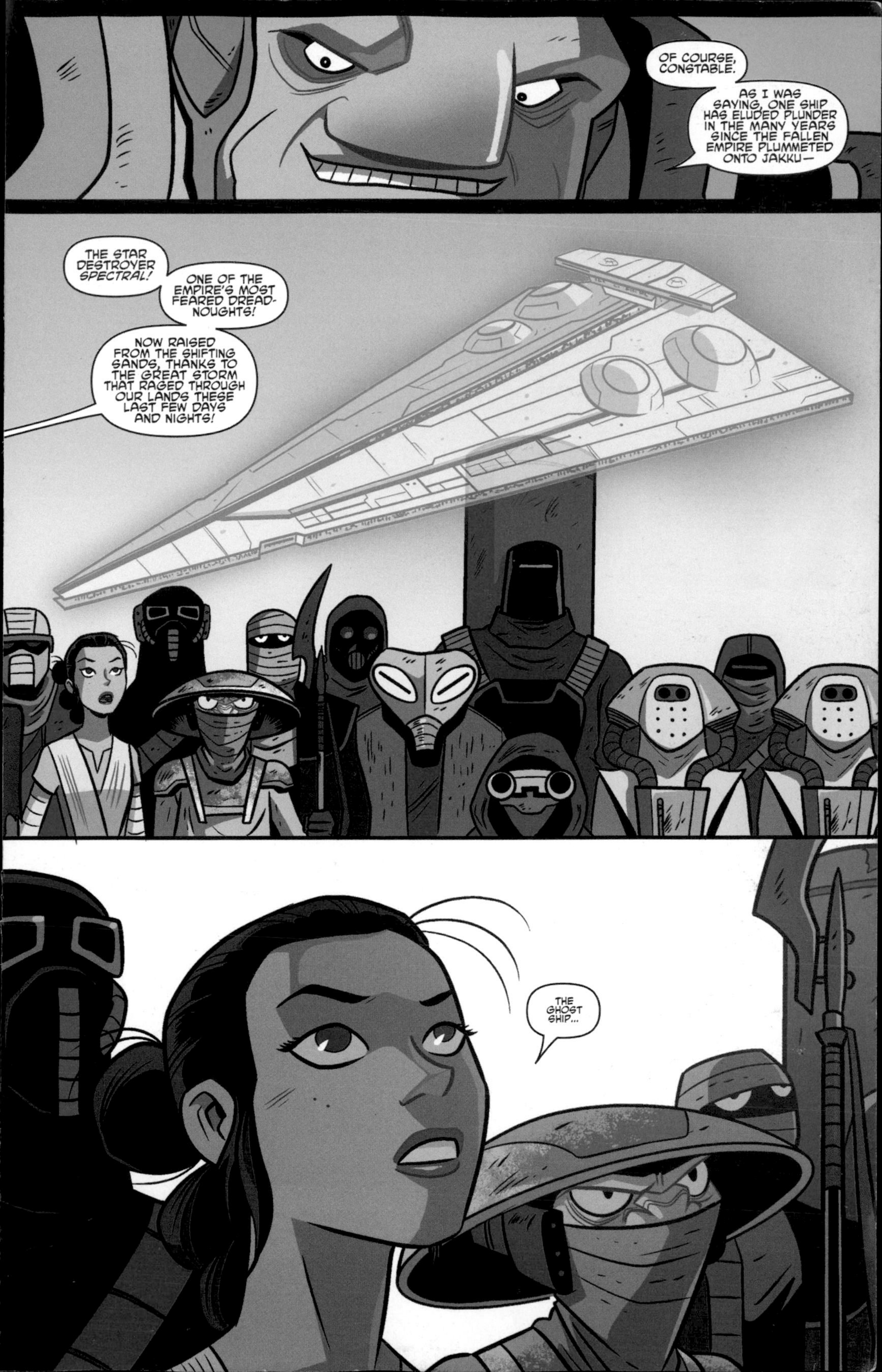
OF COURSE, CONSTABLE.
AS I WAS SAYING, ONE SHIP HAS ELUDED PLUNDER IN THE MANY YEARS SINCE THE FALLEN EMPIRE PLUMMETED ONTO JAKKU—
THE STAR DESTROYER *SPECTRAL!*
ONE OF THE EMPIRE'S MOST FEARED DREAD-NOUGHTS!
NOW RAISED FROM THE SHIFTING SANDS, THANKS TO THE GREAT STORM THAT RAGED THROUGH OUR LANDS THESE LAST FEW DAYS AND NIGHTS!
THE GHOST SHIP...

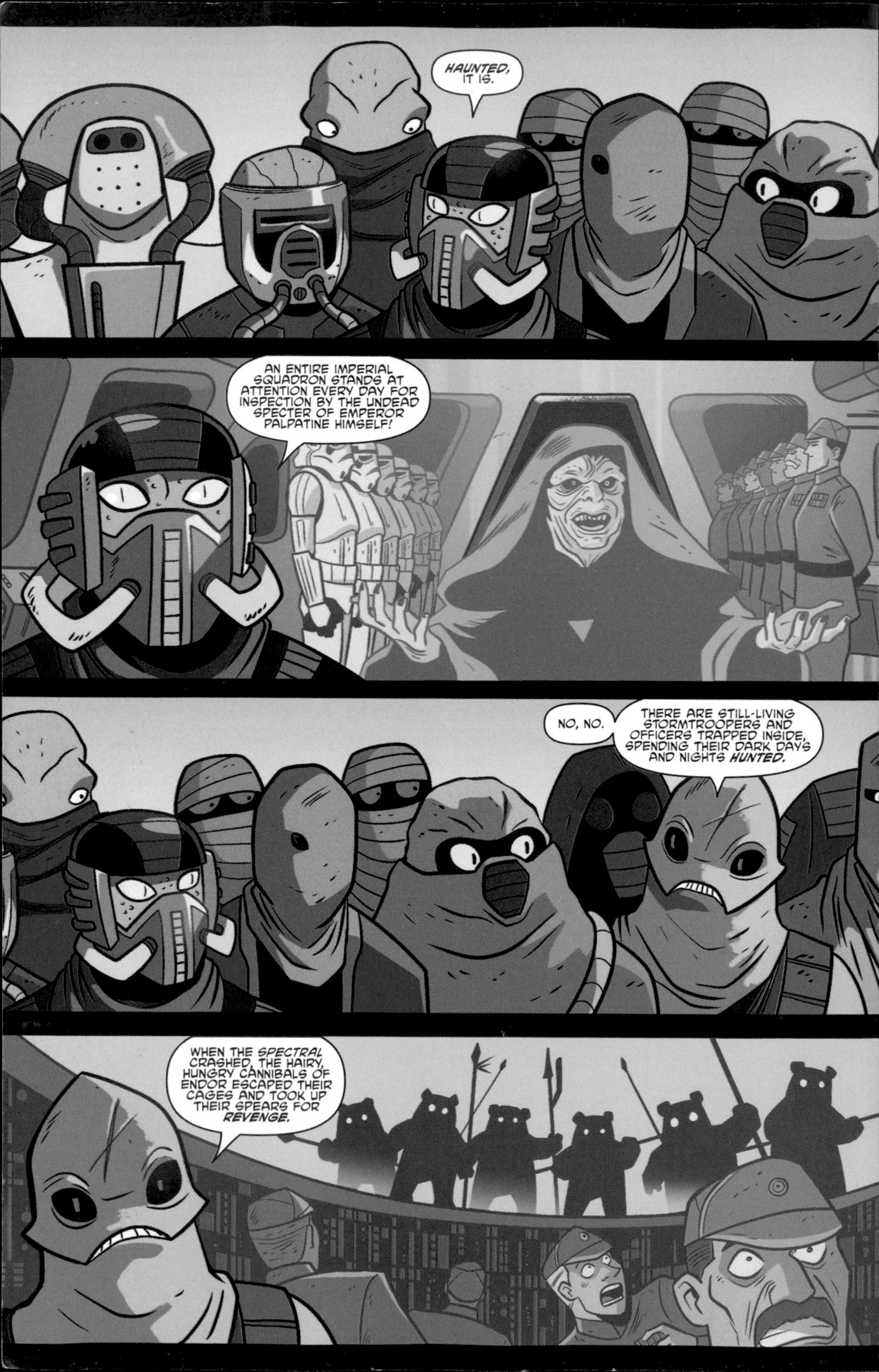
HAUNTED, IT IS.
AN ENTIRE IMPERIAL SQUADRON STANDS AT ATTENTION EVERY DAY FOR INSPECTION BY THE UNDEAD SPECTER OF EMPEROR PALPATINE HIMSELF!
NO, NO.
THERE ARE STILL-LIVING STORMTROOPERS AND OFFICERS TRAPPED INSIDE, SPENDING THEIR DARK DAYS AND NIGHTS HUNTED.
WHEN THE SPECTRAL CRASHED, THE HAIRY, HUNGRY CANNIBALS OF ENDOR ESCAPED THEIR CAGES AND TOOK UP THEIR SPEARS FOR REVENGE.

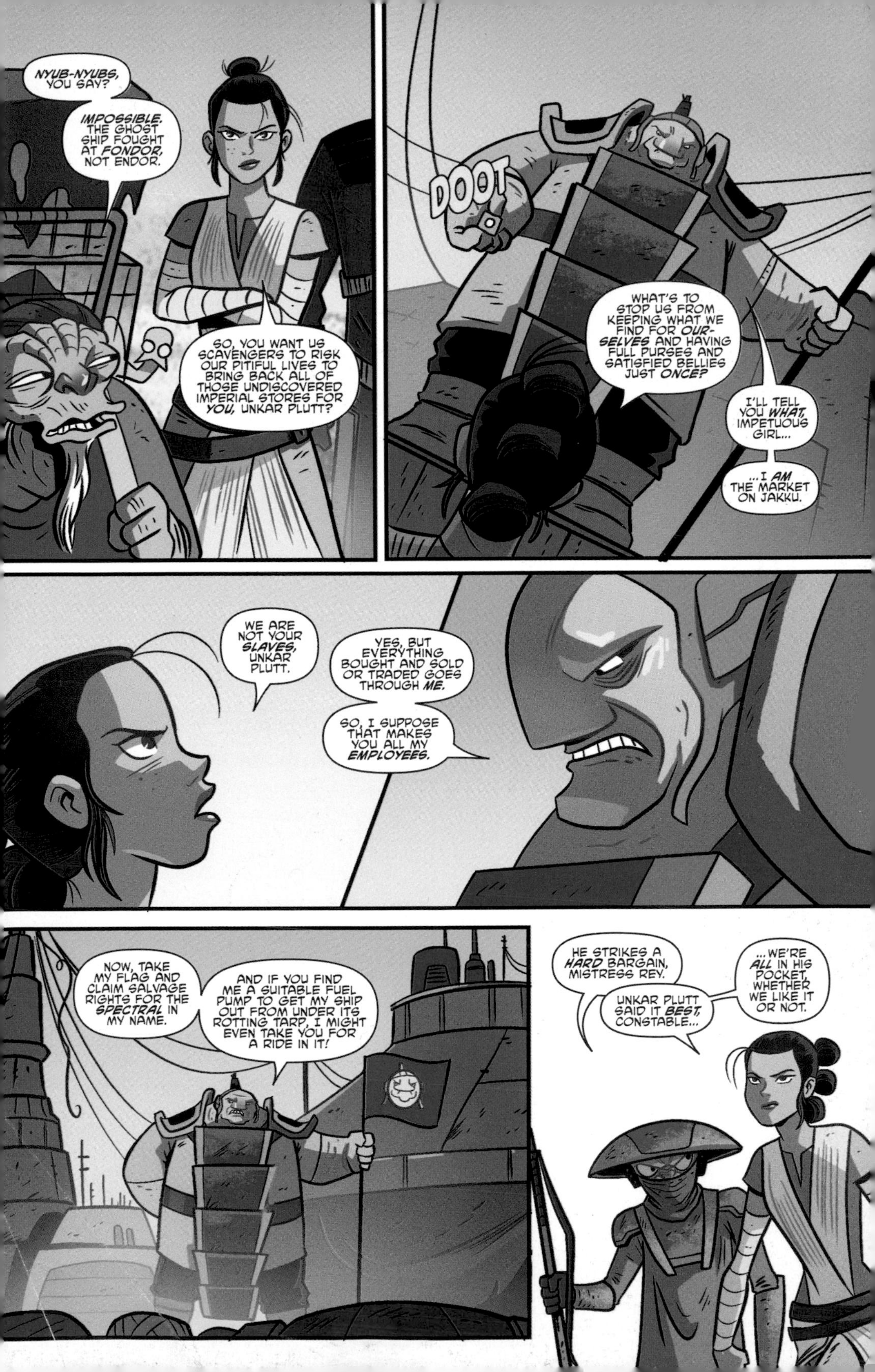
NYUB-NYUBS, YOU SAY?
IMPOSSIBLE. THE GHOST SHIP FOUGHT AT FONDOR, NOT ENDOR.
SO, YOU WANT US SCAVENGERS TO RISK OUR PITIFUL LIVES TO BRING BACK ALL OF THOSE UNDISCOVERED IMPERIAL STORES FOR YOU, UNKAR PLUTT?
DOOT
WHAT'S TO STOP US FROM KEEPING WHAT WE FIND FOR OUR-SELVES AND HAVING FULL PURSES AND SATISFIED BELLIES JUST ONCE?
I'LL TELL YOU WHAT, IMPETUOUS GIRL...
...I AM THE MARKET ON JAKKU.
WE ARE NOT YOUR SLAVES, UNKAR PLUTT.
YES, BUT EVERYTHING BOUGHT AND SOLD OR TRADED GOES THROUGH ME.
SO, I SUPPOSE THAT MAKES YOU ALL MY EMPLOYEES.
NOW, TAKE MY FLAG AND CLAIM SALVAGE RIGHTS FOR THE SPECTRAL IN MY NAME.
AND IF YOU FIND ME A SUITABLE FUEL PUMP TO GET MY SHIP OUT FROM UNDER ITS ROTTING TARP, I MIGHT EVEN TAKE YOU FOR A RIDE IN IT!
HE STRIKES A HARD BARGAIN, MISTRESS REY.
UNKAR PLUTT SAID IT BEST, CONSTABLE...
...WE'RE ALL IN HIS POCKET, WHETHER WE LIKE IT OR NOT.

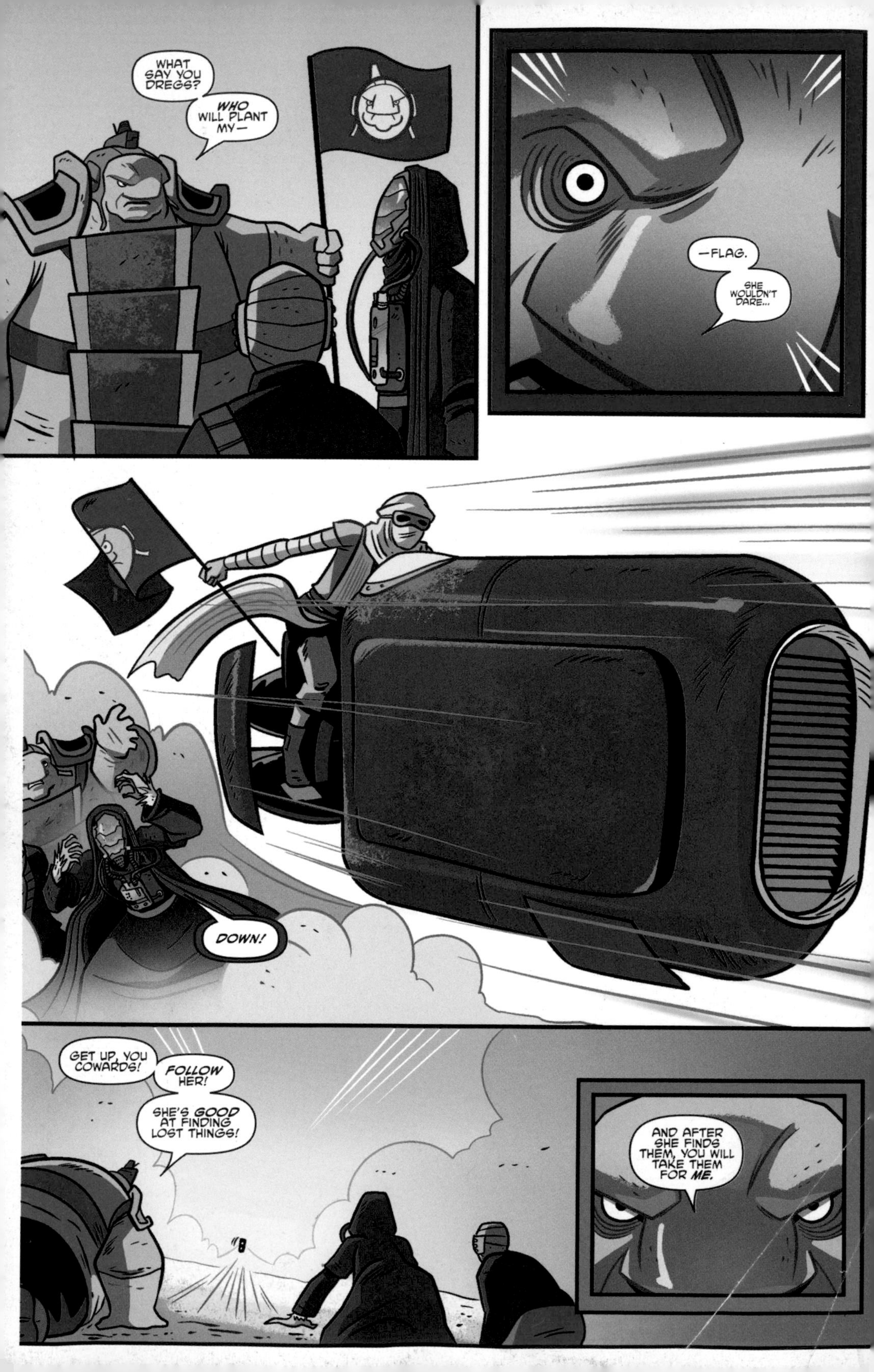
WHAT SAY YOU DREGS?
WHO WILL PLANT MY—
—FLAG.
SHE WOULDN'T DARE...
DOWN!
GET UP, YOU COWARDS!
FOLLOW HER!
SHE'S GOOD AT FINDING LOST THINGS!
AND AFTER SHE FINDS THEM, YOU WILL TAKE THEM FOR ME.

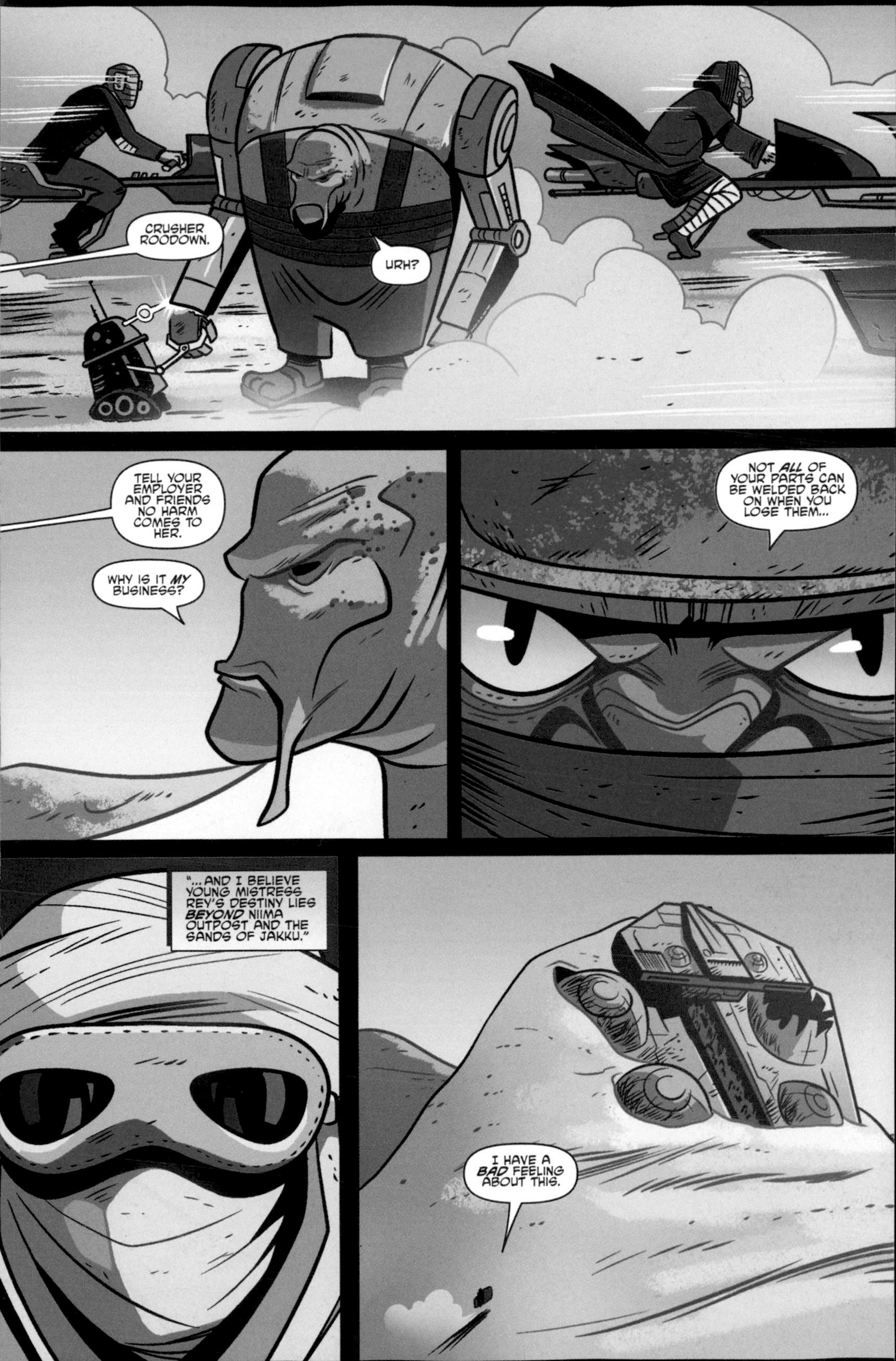
CRUSHER ROODOWN.
URH?
TELL YOUR EMPLOYER AND FRIENDS NO HARM COMES TO HER.
WHY IS IT *MY* BUSINESS?
NOT *ALL* OF YOUR PARTS CAN BE WELDED BACK ON WHEN YOU LOSE THEM...
"...AND I BELIEVE YOUNG MISTRESS REY'S DESTINY LIES *BEYOND* NIIMA OUTPOST AND THE SANDS OF JAKKU."
I HAVE A *BAD* FEELING ABOUT THIS.

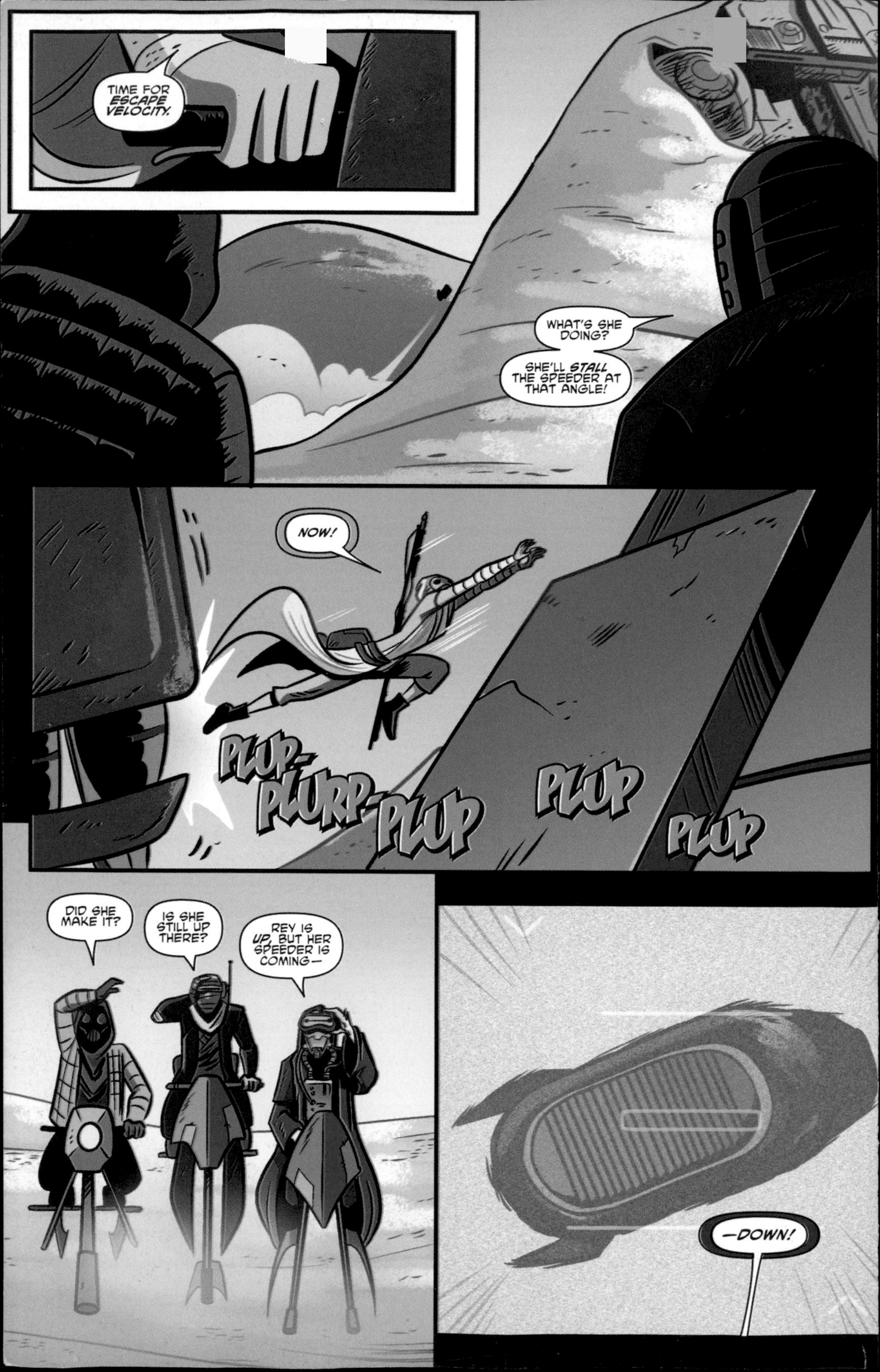
TIME FOR *ESCAPE VELOCITY.*
WHAT'S SHE DOING?
SHE'LL *STALL* THE SPEEDER AT THAT ANGLE!
NOW!
PLUP-PLURP-PLUP
PLUP
PLUP
DID SHE MAKE IT?
IS SHE STILL UP THERE?
REY IS *UP,* BUT HER SPEEDER IS COMING—
—*DOWN!*

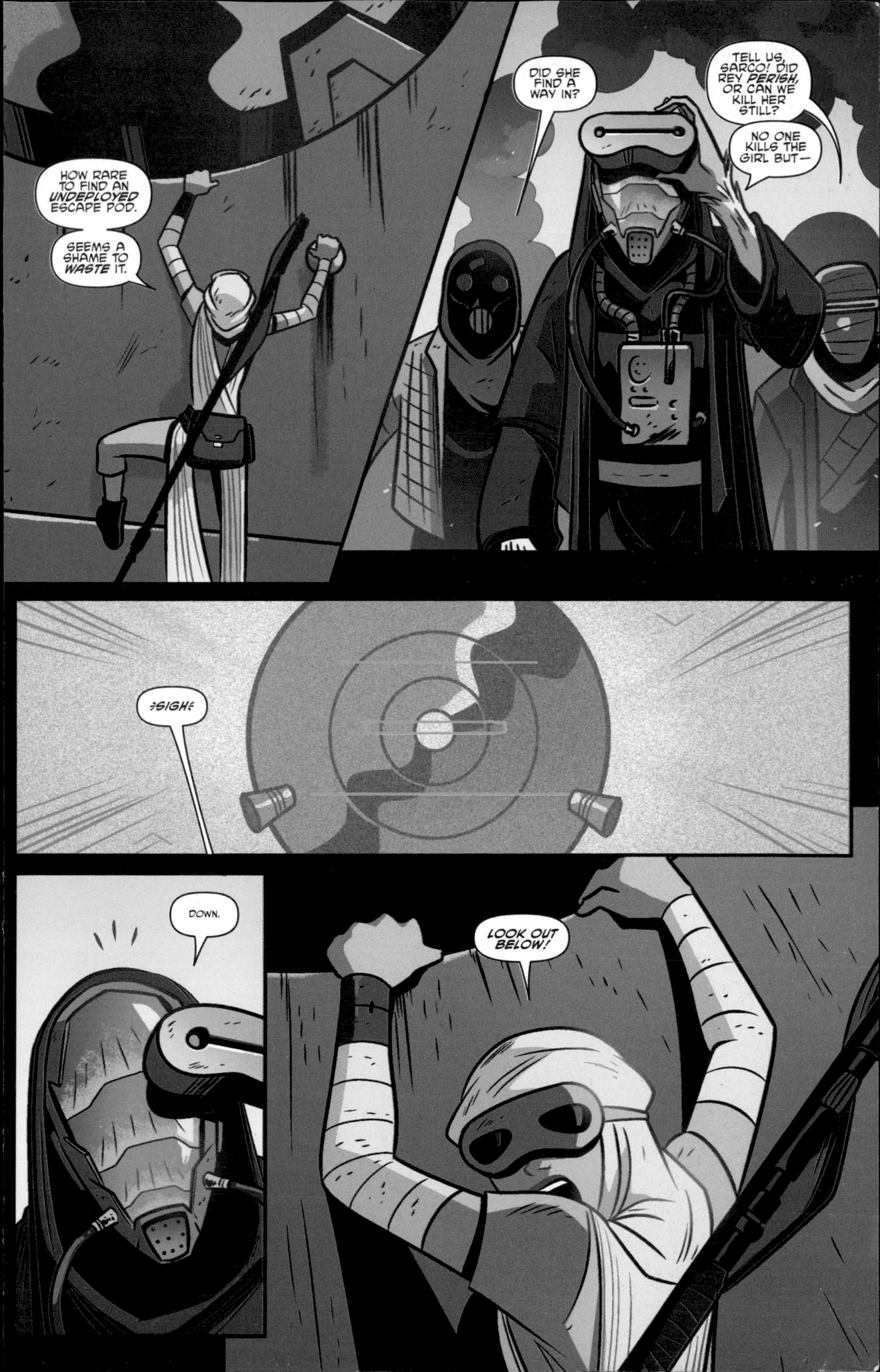
HOW RARE TO FIND AN UNDEPLOYED ESCAPE POD.
SEEMS A SHAME TO WASTE IT.
DID SHE FIND A WAY IN?
TELL US, SARCO! DID REY PERISH, OR CAN WE KILL HER STILL?
NO ONE KILLS THE GIRL BUT—
SIGH
DOWN.
LOOK OUT BELOW!

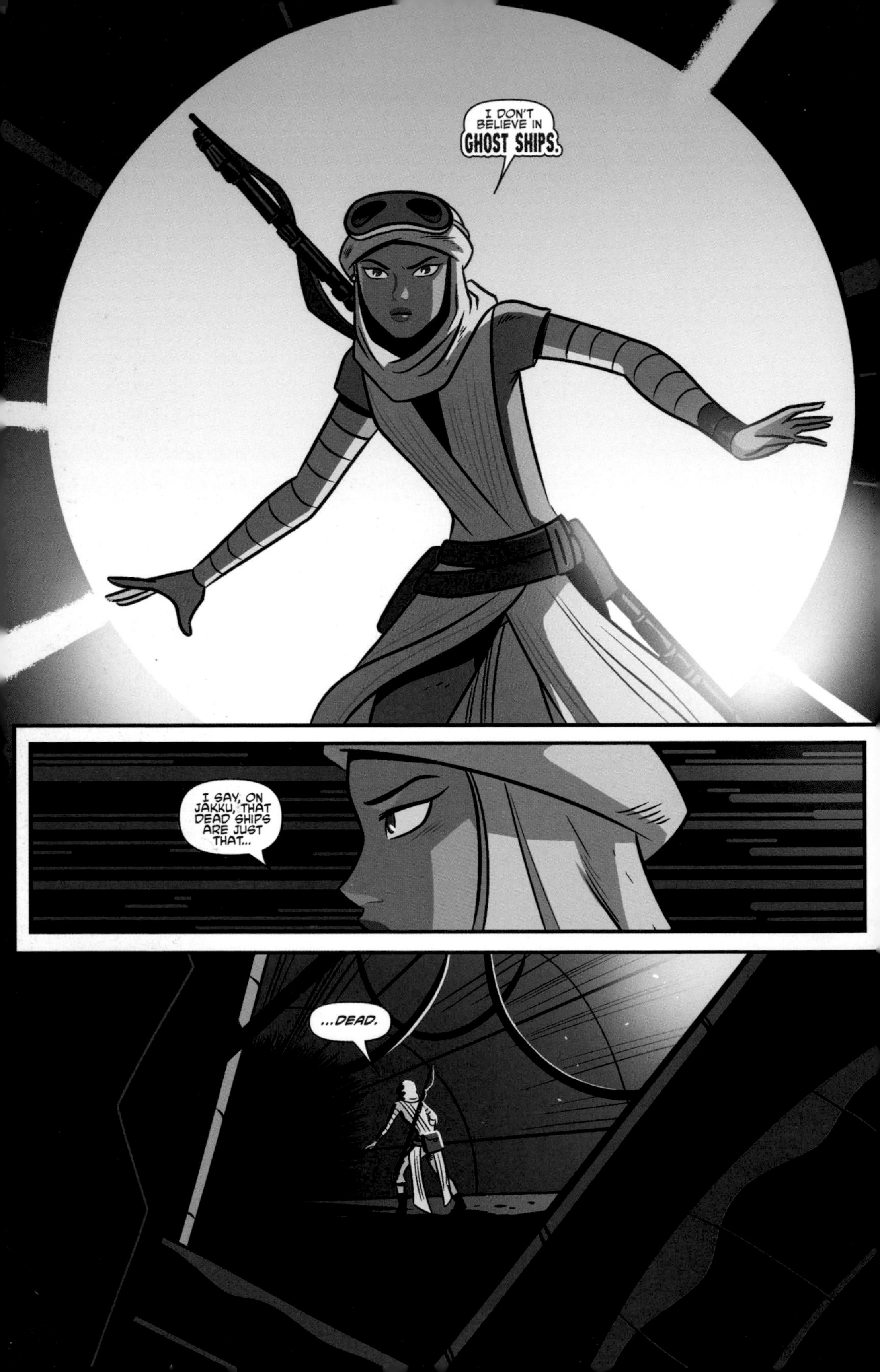
I DON'T BELIEVE IN GHOST SHIPS.
I SAY, ON JAKKU, THAT DEAD SHIPS ARE JUST THAT...
...DEAD.

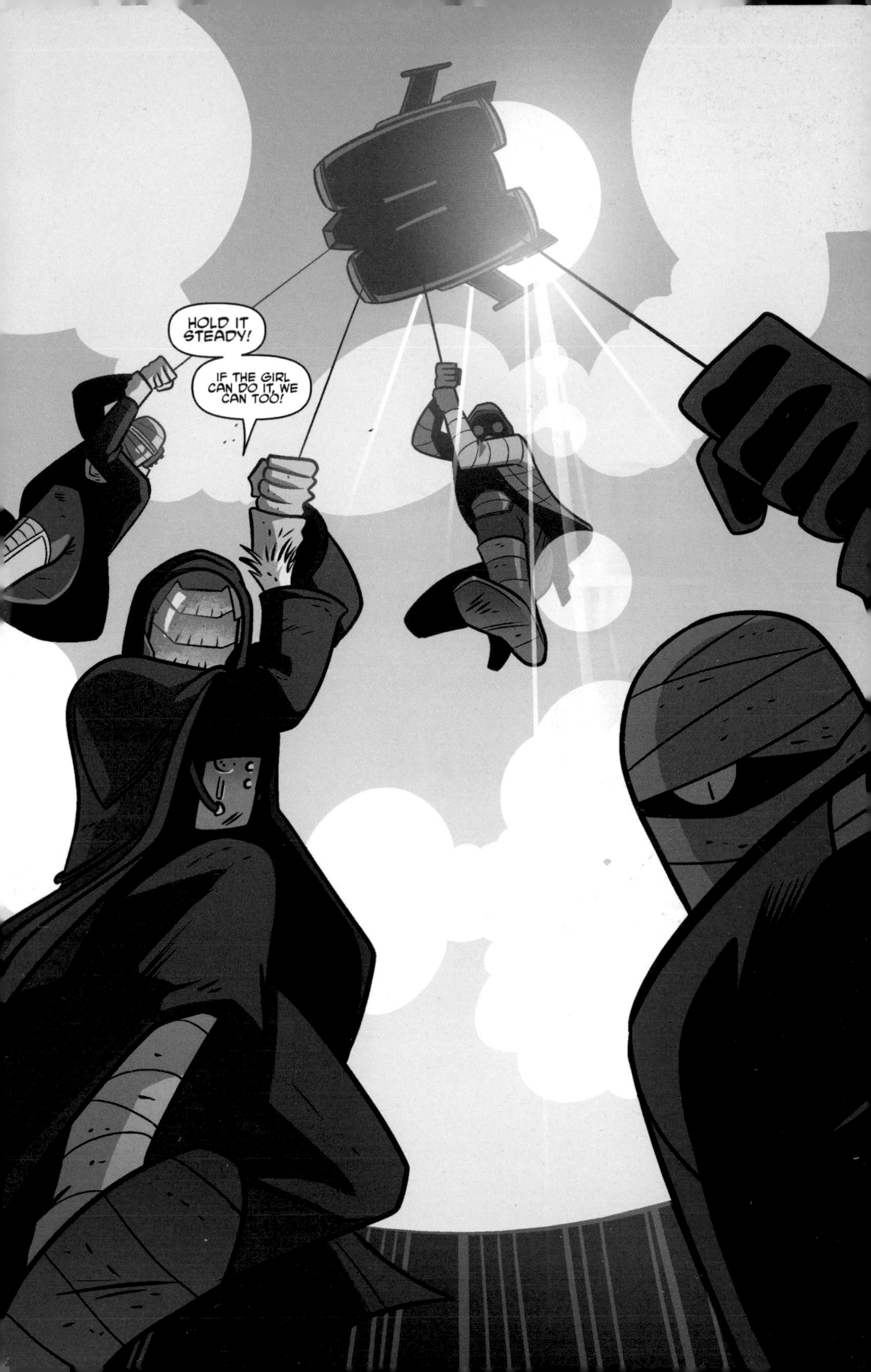
HOLD IT STEADY!
IF THE GIRL CAN DO IT, WE CAN TOO!

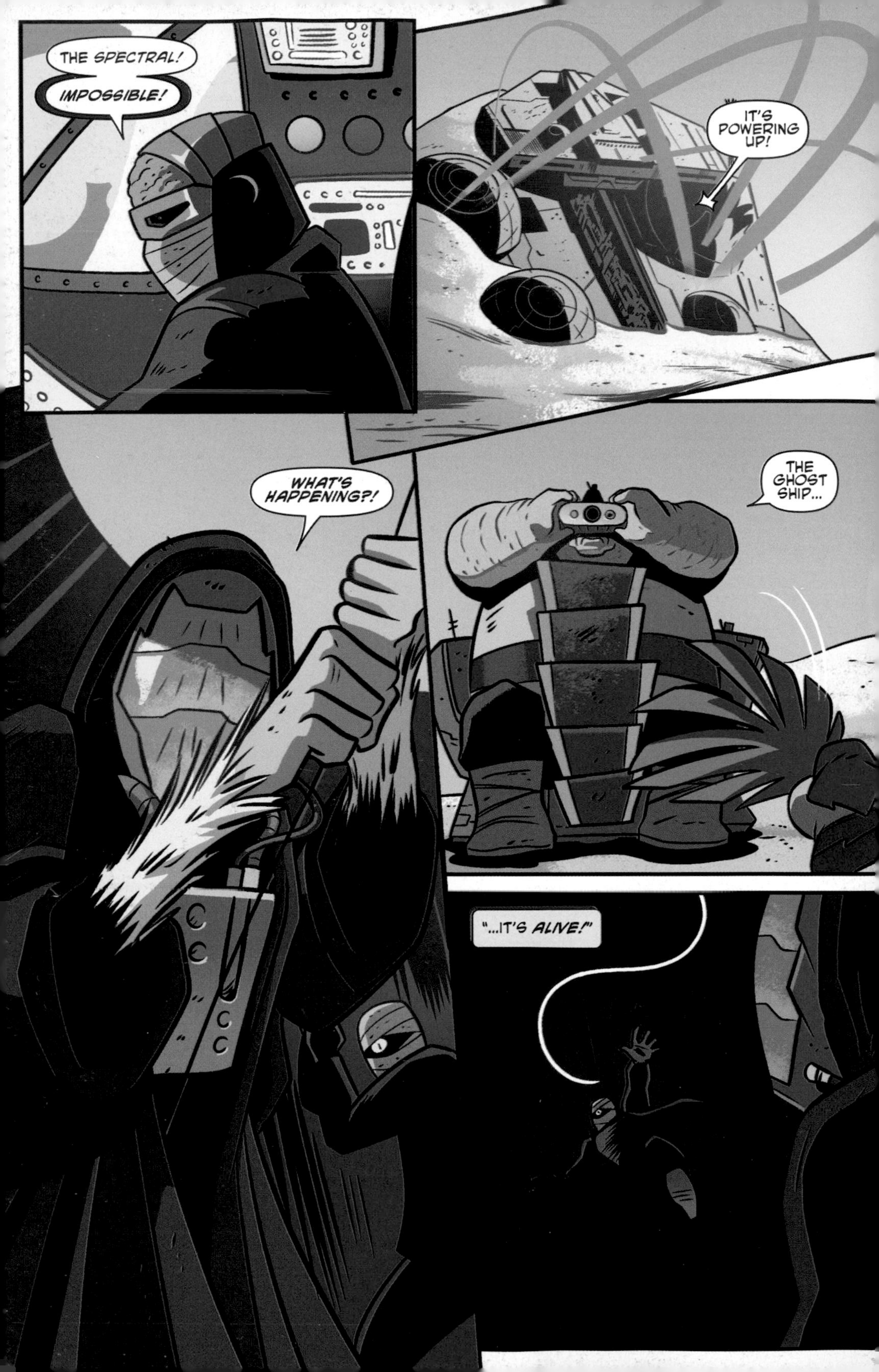
THE SPECTRAL!
IMPOSSIBLE!
IT'S POWERING UP!
WHAT'S HAPPENING?!
THE GHOST SHIP...
"...IT'S ALIVE!"

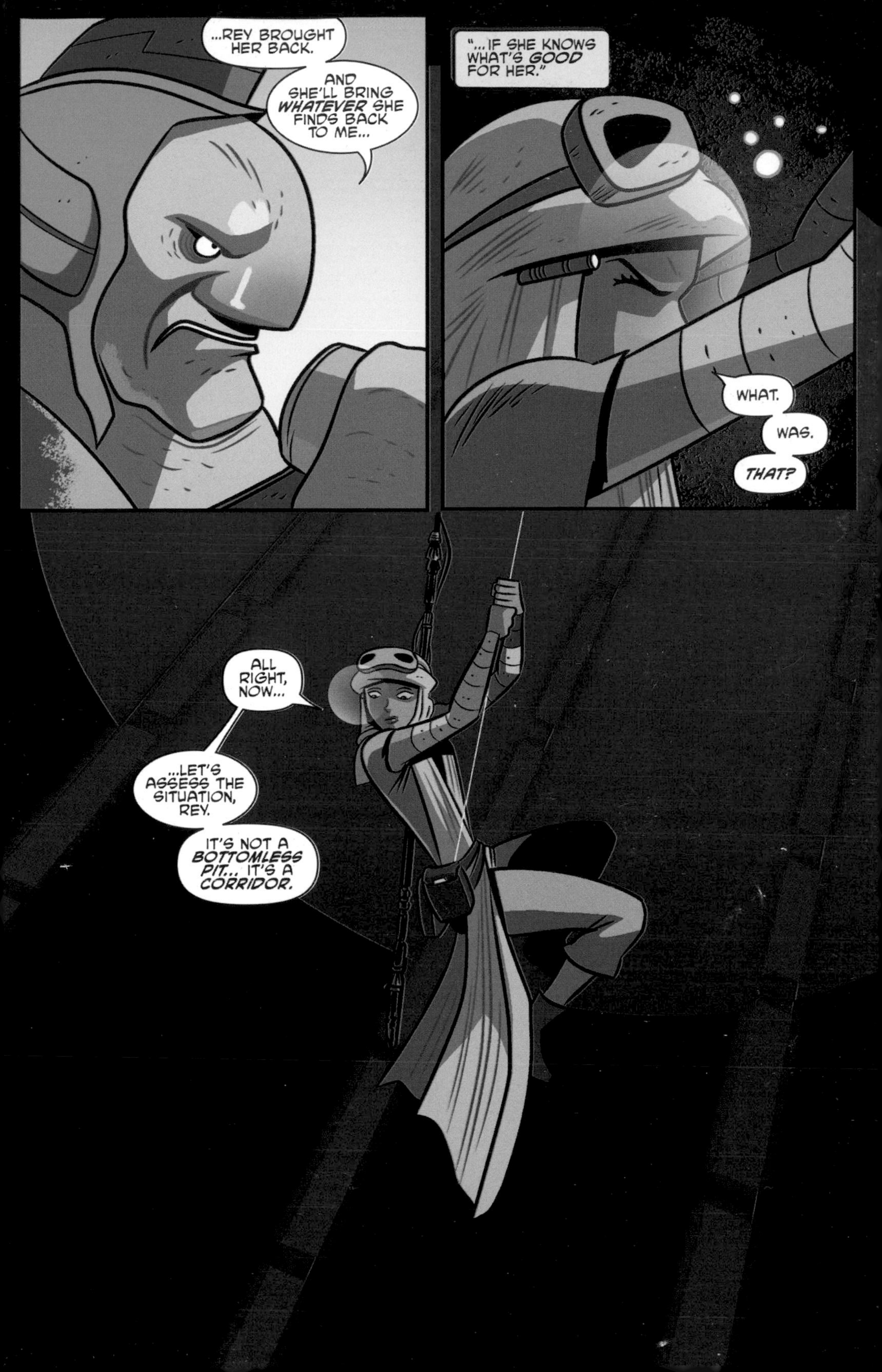
...REY BROUGHT HER BACK.
AND SHE'LL BRING WHATEVER SHE FINDS BACK TO ME...
"...IF SHE KNOWS WHAT'S GOOD FOR HER."
WHAT.
WAS.
THAT?
ALL RIGHT, NOW...
...LET'S ASSESS THE SITUATION, REY.
IT'S NOT A BOTTOMLESS PIT... IT'S A CORRIDOR.

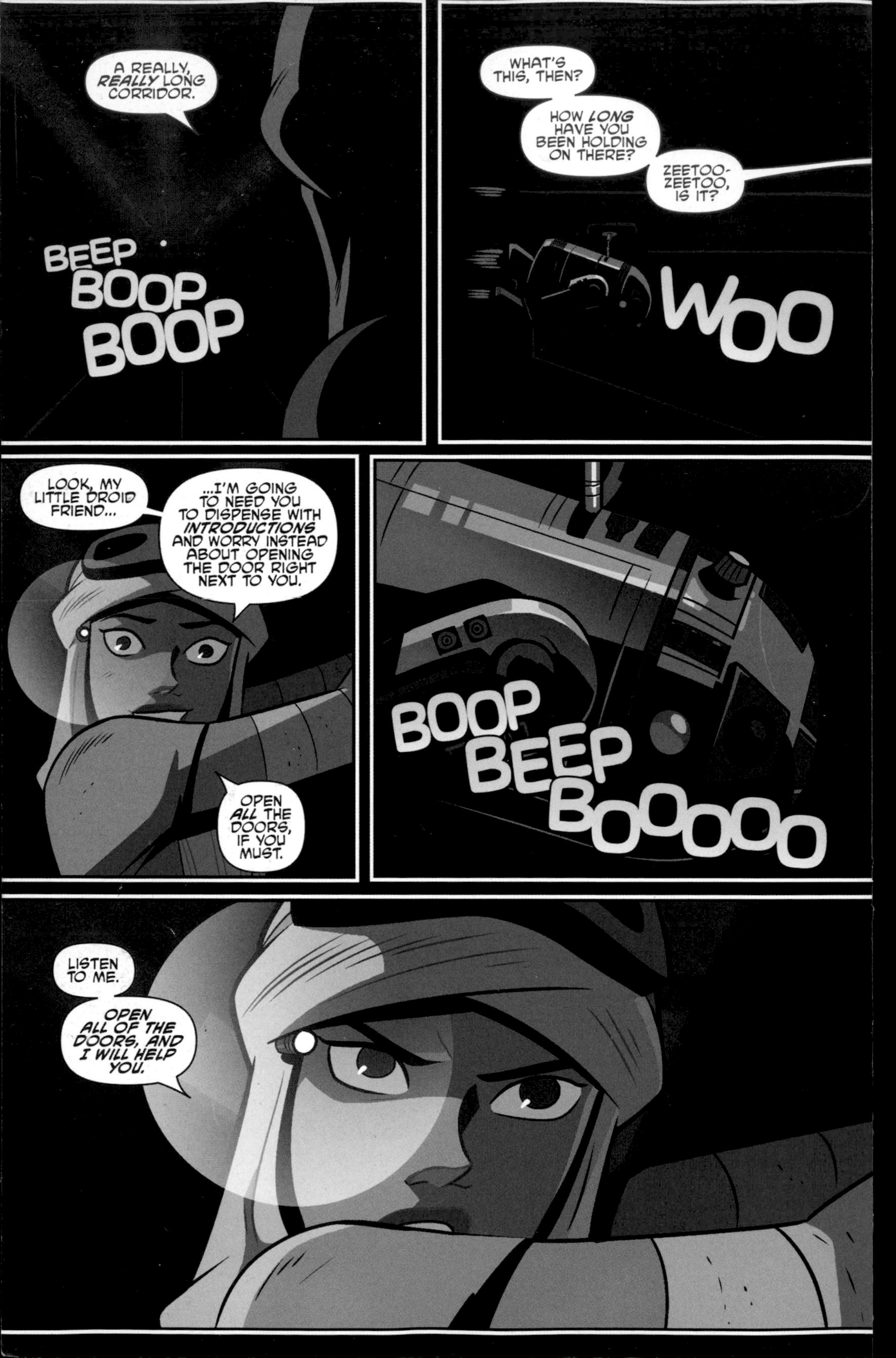
A REALLY, REALLY LONG CORRIDOR.
BEEP BOOP BOOP
WHAT'S THIS, THEN?
HOW LONG HAVE YOU BEEN HOLDING ON THERE?
ZEETOO-ZEETOO, IS IT?
WOO
LOOK, MY LITTLE DROID FRIEND...
...I'M GOING TO NEED YOU TO DISPENSE WITH INTRODUCTIONS AND WORRY INSTEAD ABOUT OPENING THE DOOR RIGHT NEXT TO YOU.
OPEN ALL THE DOORS, IF YOU MUST.
BOOP BEEP BOOOOOO
LISTEN TO ME.
OPEN ALL OF THE DOORS, AND I WILL HELP YOU.

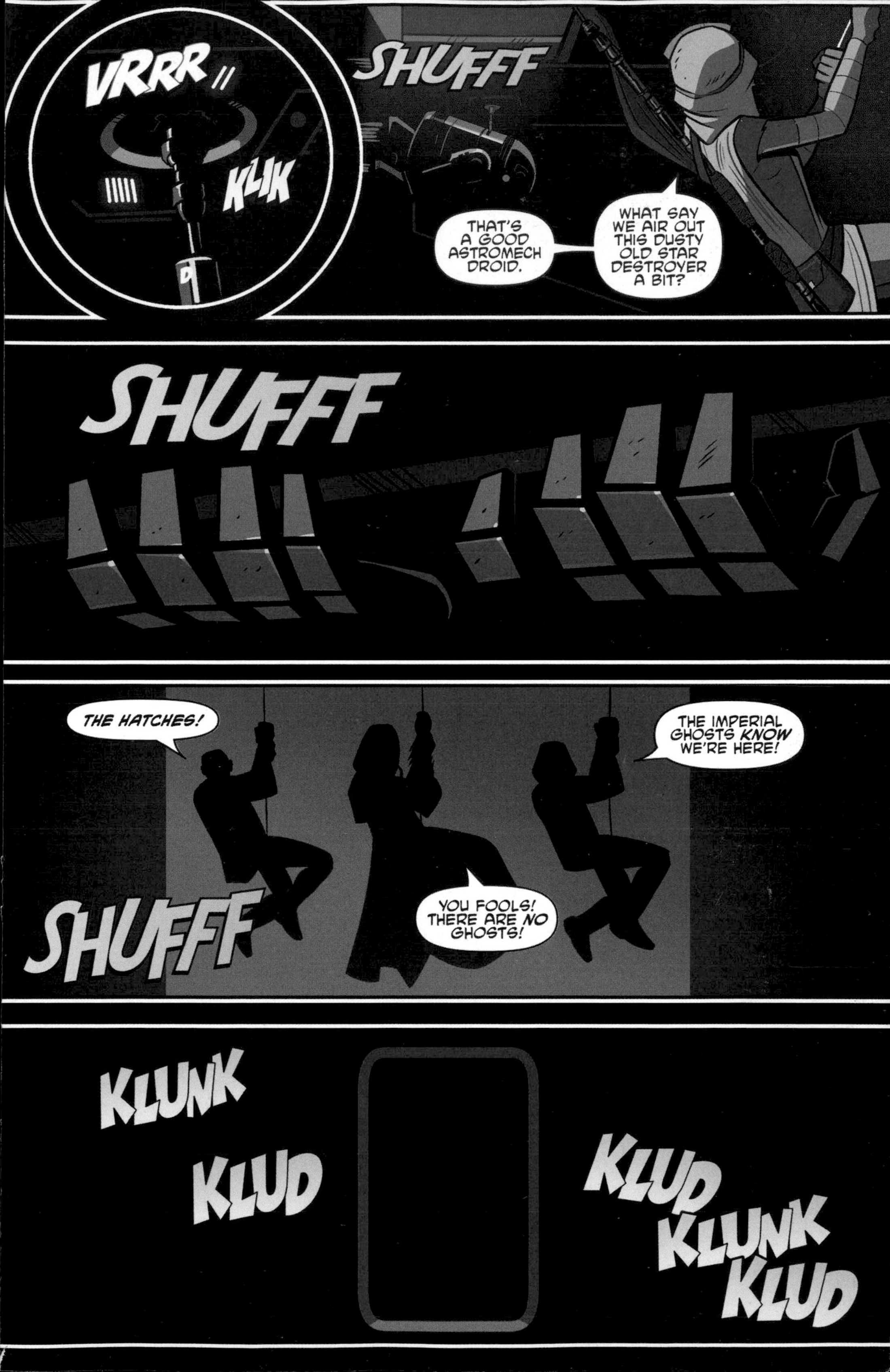
VRRR
KLIK
SHUFFF
WHAT SAY WE AIR OUT THIS DUSTY OLD STAR DESTROYER A BIT?
THAT'S A GOOD ASTROMECH DROID.
SHUFFF
THE HATCHES!
THE IMPERIAL GHOSTS *KNOW* WE'RE HERE!
SHUFFF
YOU FOOLS! THERE ARE *NO* GHOSTS!
KLUNK
KLUD
KLUD
KLUNK
KLUD

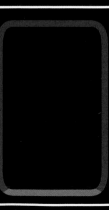

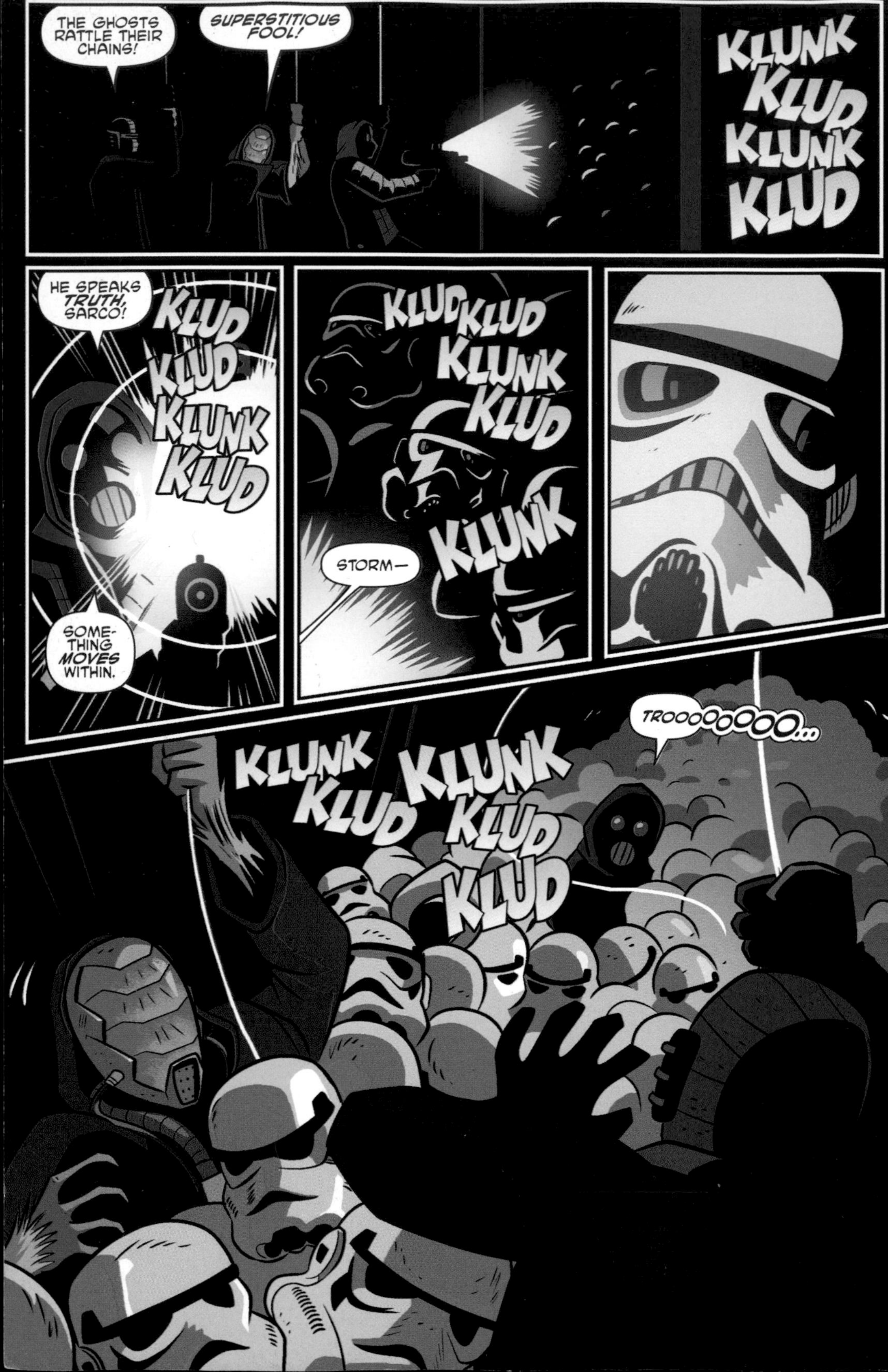
THE GHOSTS RATTLE THEIR CHAINS!
SUPERSTITIOUS FOOL!
KLUNK KLUD KLUNK KLUD
HE SPEAKS TRUTH, SARCO!
KLUD KLUD KLUNK KLUD
SOME-THING MOVES WITHIN.
KLUD KLUD KLUNK KLUD
STORM—
KLUNK
TROOOOOOOO...
KLUNK KLUD
KLUNK KLUD KLUD

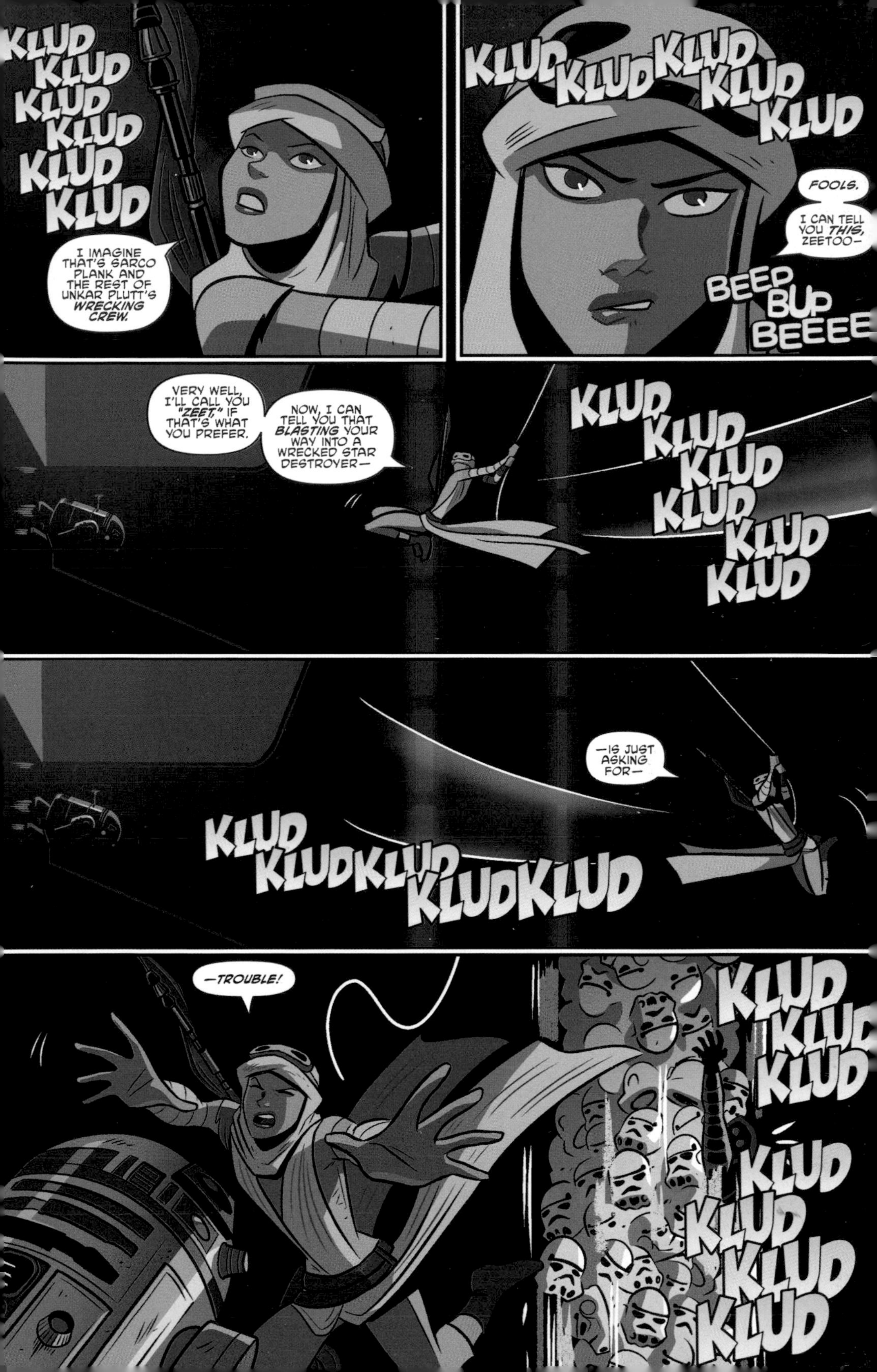
KLUD KLUD KLUD KLUD KLUD KLUD
I IMAGINE THAT'S SARCO PLANK AND THE REST OF UNKAR PLUTT'S *WRECKING CREW.*
KLUD KLUD KLUD KLUD KLUD
FOOLS.
I CAN TELL YOU *THIS,* ZEETOO—
BEEP BUP BEEEE
VERY WELL, I'LL CALL YOU *"ZEET,"* IF THAT'S WHAT YOU PREFER.
NOW, I CAN TELL YOU THAT *BLASTING* YOUR WAY INTO A WRECKED STAR DESTROYER—
KLUD KLUD KLUD KLUD KLUD KLUD
—IS JUST ASKING FOR—
KLUD KLUDKLUD KLUDKLUD
—TROUBLE!
KLUD KLUD KLUD
KLUD KLUD KLUD KLUD

BA DOOP

YOU SAID IT, ZEET.

SO.

WITH THOSE BRIGHT FLASHY COLORS, YOU DON'T STRIKE ME AS AN *IMPERIAL* ASTROMECH.

BEE BOO BEE BOO

OH, YOU'RE A *REBEL* THEN?

OF COURSE. NO DOUBT A *SABOTEUR* FROM THE GRAND OLD DAYS OF THE REBELLION.

ALL THOSE TALES OF IMMORTAL JEDI WARRIORS AND PLANET-SIZED DEATH STARS AND—

—TOP-SECRET PLANS.

VRRRT

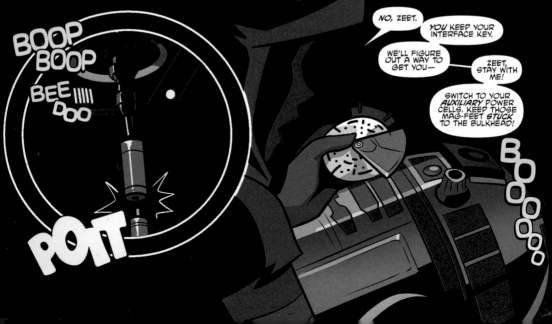

BOOP BOOP BEE DOO

POTT

NO, ZEET.

YOU KEEP YOUR INTERFACE KEY.

WE'LL FIGURE OUT A WAY TO GET YOU—

ZEET, STAY WITH ME!

SWITCH TO YOUR *AUXILIARY* POWER CELLS. KEEP THOSE MAG-FEET *STUCK* TO THE BULKHEAD!

BOOOO

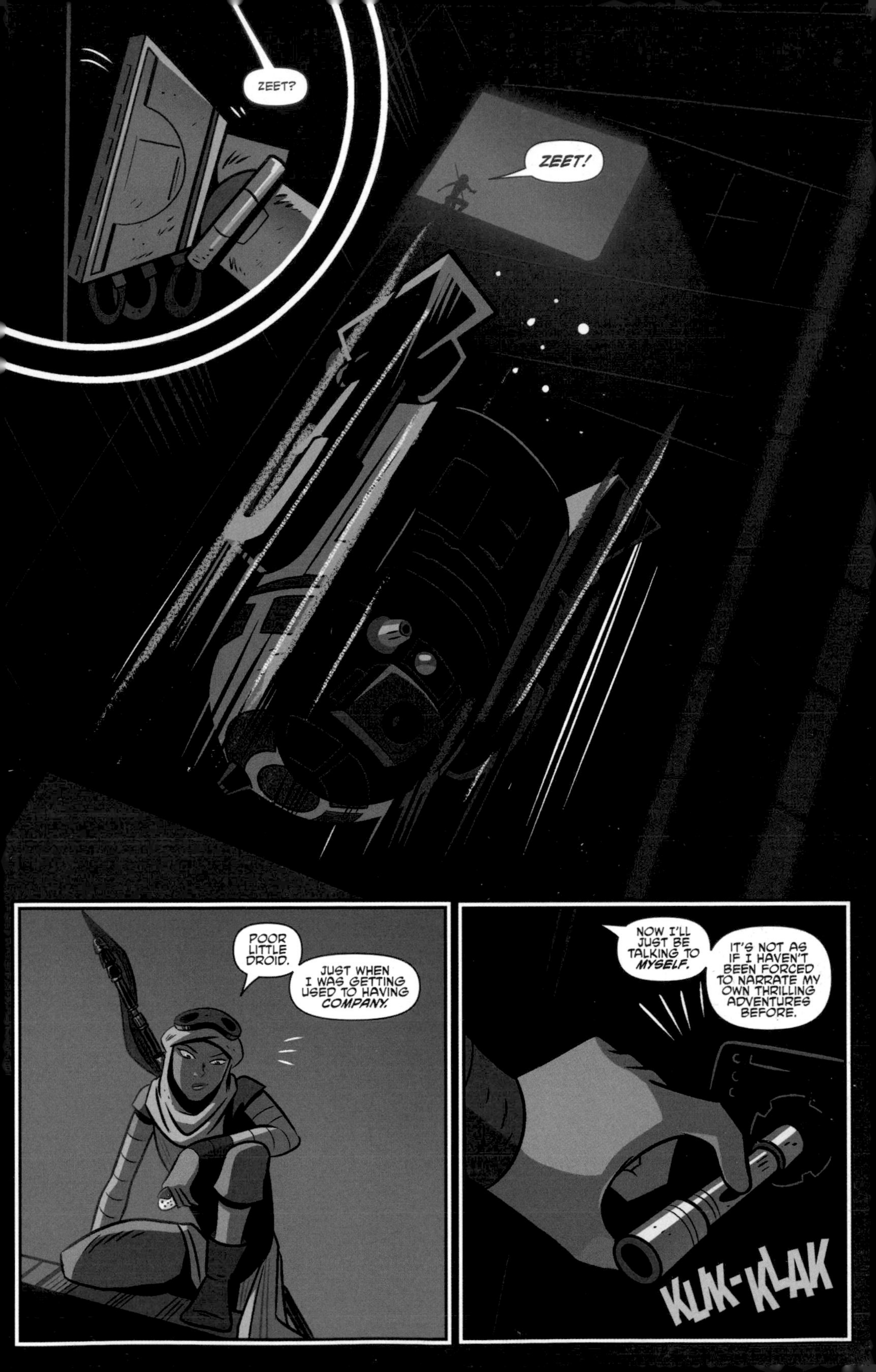

ZEET?
ZEET!
POOR LITTLE DROID.
JUST WHEN I WAS GETTING USED TO HAVING COMPANY.
NOW I'LL JUST BE TALKING TO MYSELF.
IT'S NOT AS IF I HAVEN'T BEEN FORCED TO NARRATE MY OWN THRILLING ADVENTURES BEFORE.
KLIK-KLAK

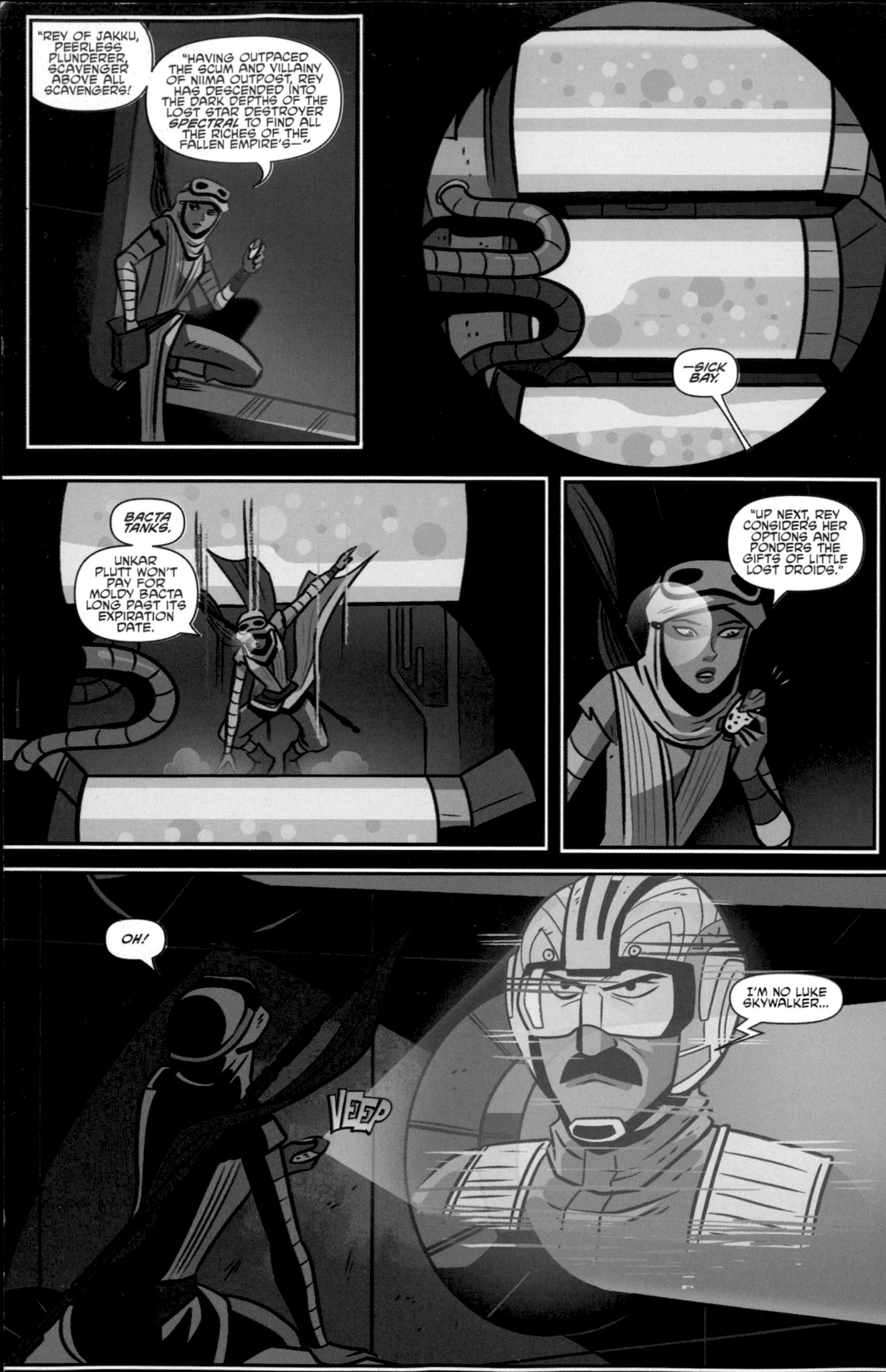
"REY OF JAKKU, PEERLESS PLUNDERER, SCAVENGER ABOVE ALL SCAVENGERS!
"HAVING OUTPACED THE SCUM AND VILLAINY OF NIIMA OUTPOST, REY HAS DESCENDED INTO THE DARK DEPTHS OF THE LOST STAR DESTROYER SPECTRAL TO FIND ALL THE RICHES OF THE FALLEN EMPIRE'S—"
—SICK BAY.
BACTA TANKS.
UNKAR PLUTT WON'T PAY FOR MOLDY BACTA LONG PAST ITS EXPIRATION DATE.
"UP NEXT, REY CONSIDERS HER OPTIONS AND PONDERS THE GIFTS OF LITTLE LOST DROIDS."
OH!
VEEP
I'M NO LUKE SKYWALKER...

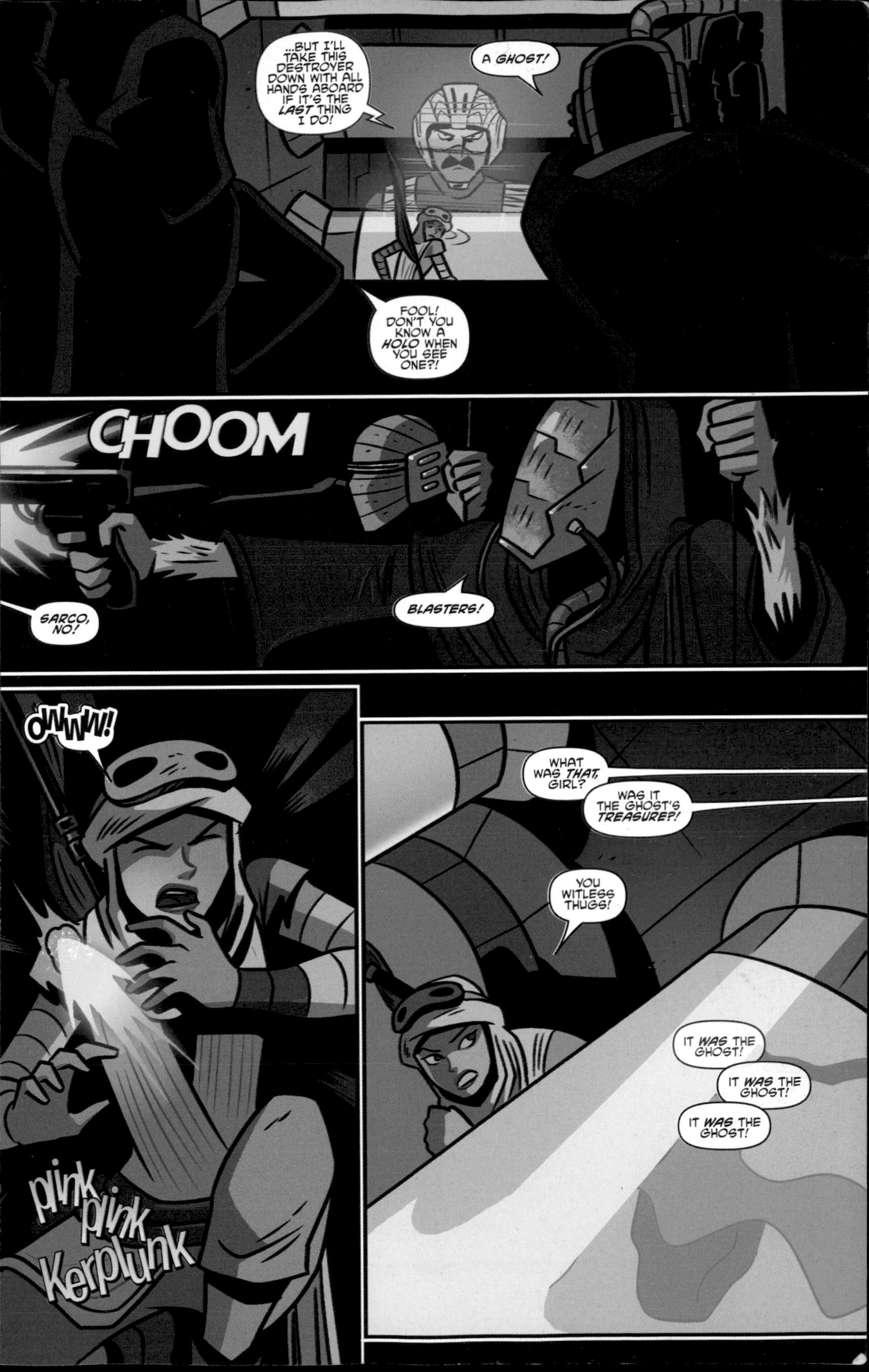
...BUT I'LL TAKE THIS DESTROYER DOWN WITH ALL HANDS ABOARD IF IT'S THE LAST THING I DO!
A GHOST!
FOOL! DON'T YOU KNOW A HOLO WHEN YOU SEE ONE?!
CHOOM
SARCO, NO!
BLASTERS!
OWWW!
plink plink Kerplunk
WHAT WAS THAT, GIRL?
WAS IT THE GHOST'S TREASURE?!
YOU WITLESS THUGS!
IT WAS THE GHOST!
IT WAS THE GHOST!
IT WAS THE GHOST!

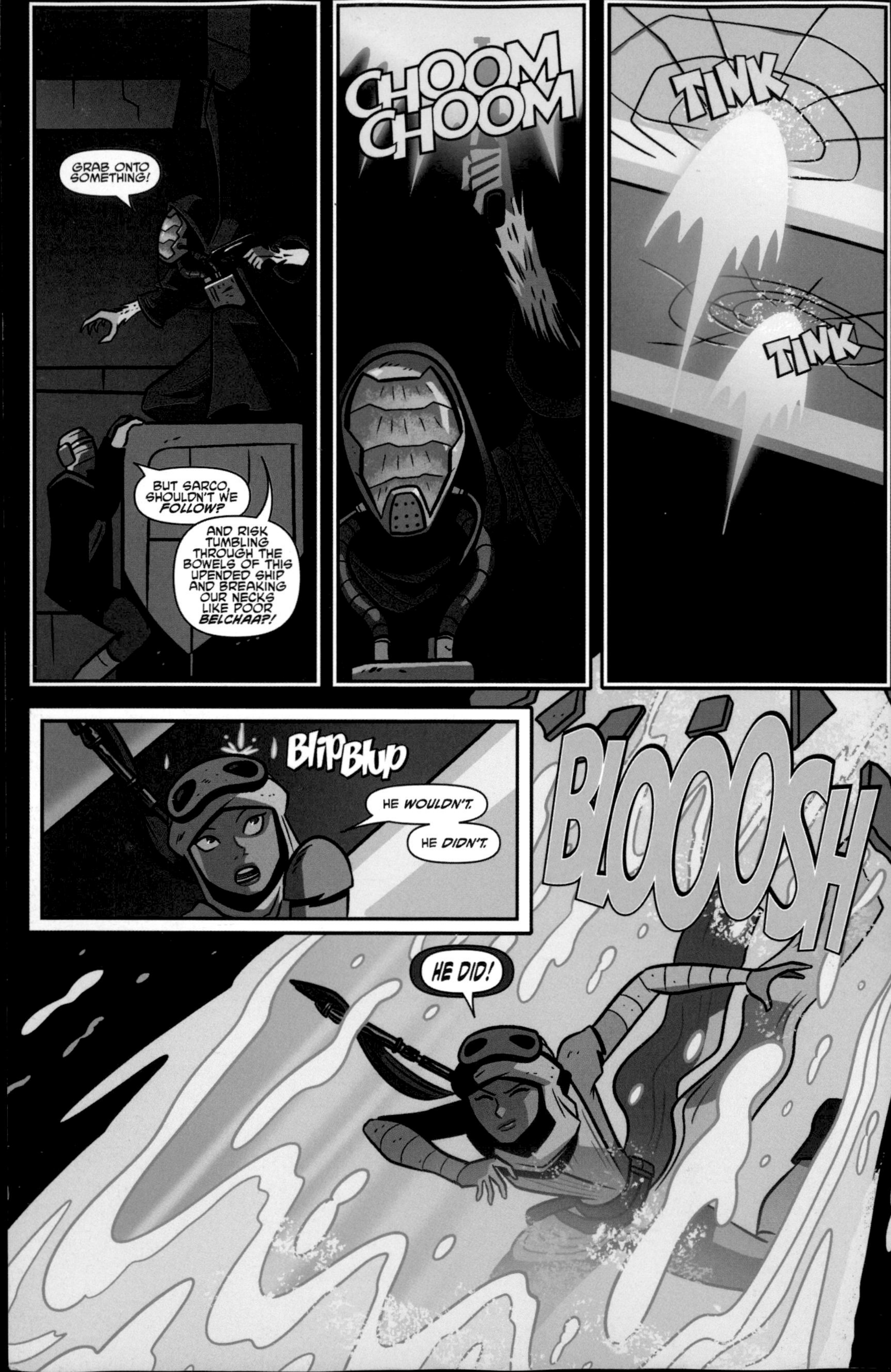
GRAB ONTO SOMETHING!
BUT SARCO, SHOULDN'T WE *FOLLOW?*
AND RISK TUMBLING THROUGH THE BOWELS OF THIS UPENDED SHIP AND BREAKING OUR NECKS LIKE POOR *BELCHAA?!*
CHOOM CHOOM
TINK
TINK
BlipBlup
HE *WOULDN'T.*
HE *DIDN'T.*
BLOOOSH
HE DID!

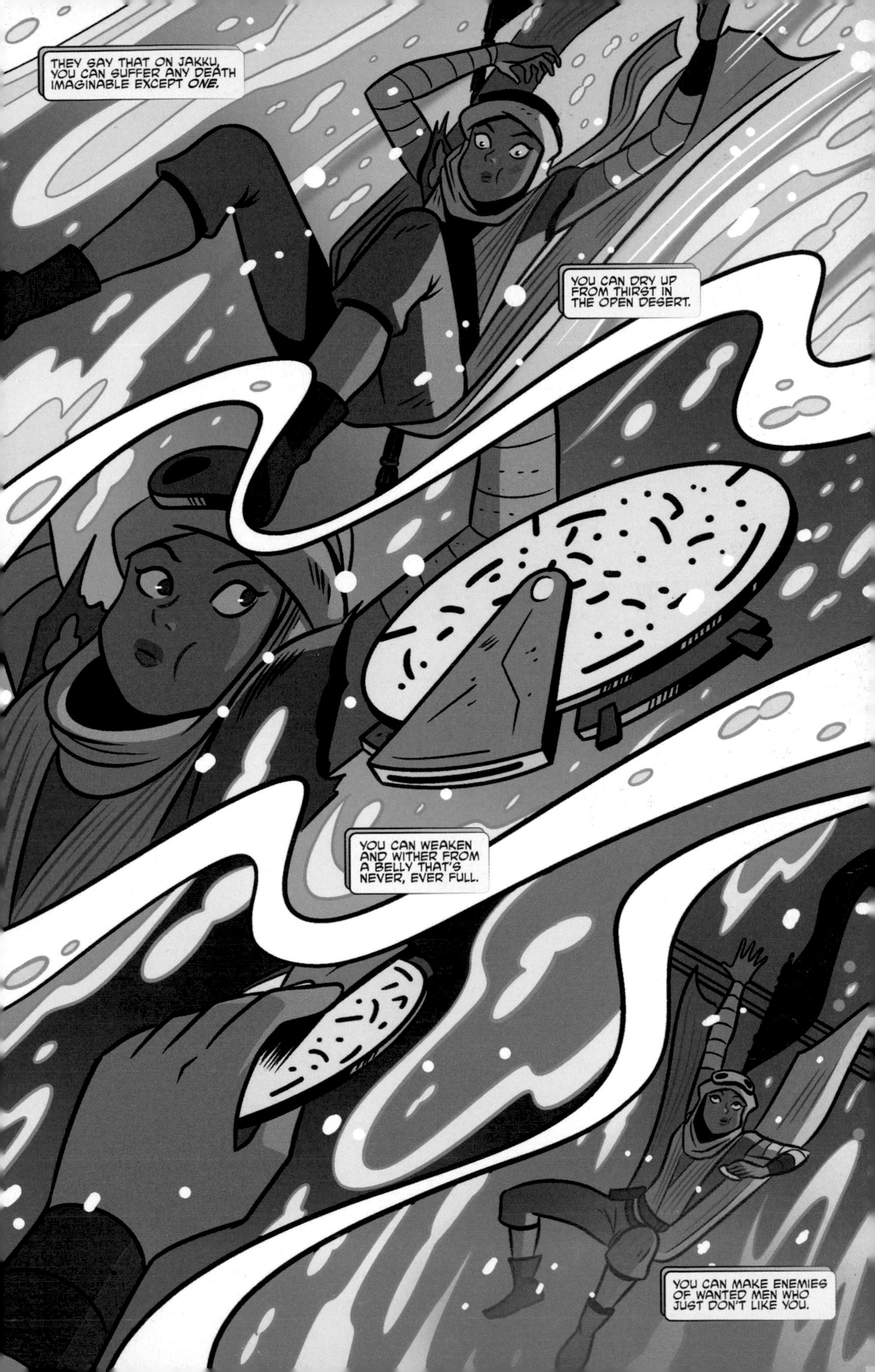
THEY SAY THAT ON JAKKU, YOU CAN SUFFER ANY DEATH IMAGINABLE EXCEPT *ONE.*
YOU CAN DRY UP FROM THIRST IN THE OPEN DESERT.
YOU CAN WEAKEN AND WITHER FROM A BELLY THAT'S NEVER, EVER FULL.
YOU CAN MAKE ENEMIES OF WANTED MEN WHO JUST DON'T LIKE YOU.

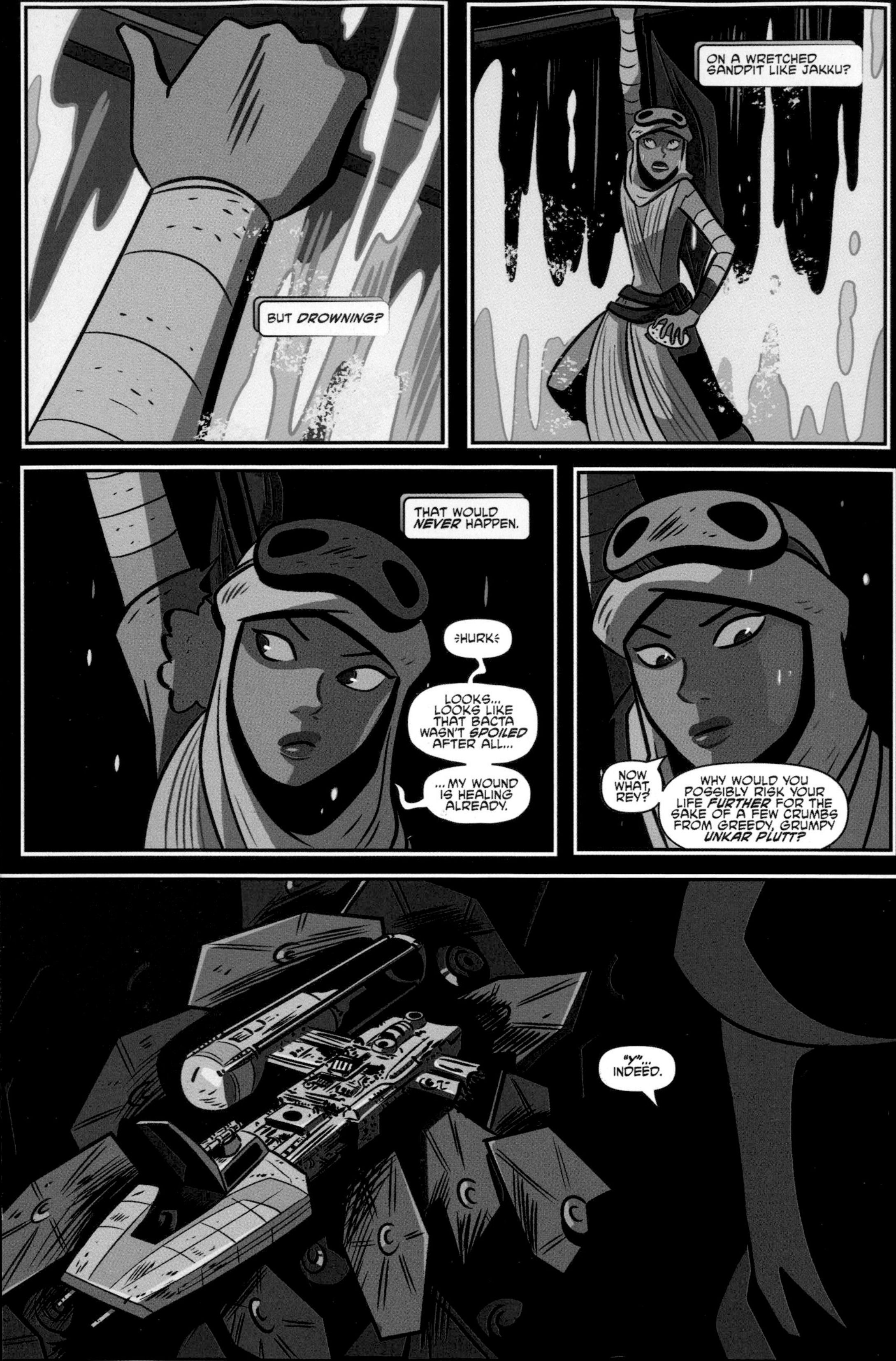
BUT DROWNING?
ON A WRETCHED SANDPIT LIKE JAKKU?
THAT WOULD NEVER HAPPEN.
HURK
LOOKS... LOOKS LIKE THAT BACTA WASN'T SPOILED AFTER ALL...
...MY WOUND IS HEALING ALREADY.
NOW WHAT, REY?
WHY WOULD YOU POSSIBLY RISK YOUR LIFE FURTHER FOR THE SAKE OF A FEW CRUMBS FROM GREEDY, GRUMPY UNKAR PLUTT?
"Y"... INDEED.

A LONG TIME AGO ON JAKKU...
...IN THE LAST DAYS OF THE GALACTIC EMPIRE...
THE SHIP GUARDS THE EMPIRE.
AND I GUARD THE SHIP.
...THEY SAY THAT MOST STAR DESTROYER COMMAND DECK OFFICERS WENT DOWN WITH THEIR SHIPS TO PROVE THEIR LOYALTY TO EMPEROR PALPATINE.

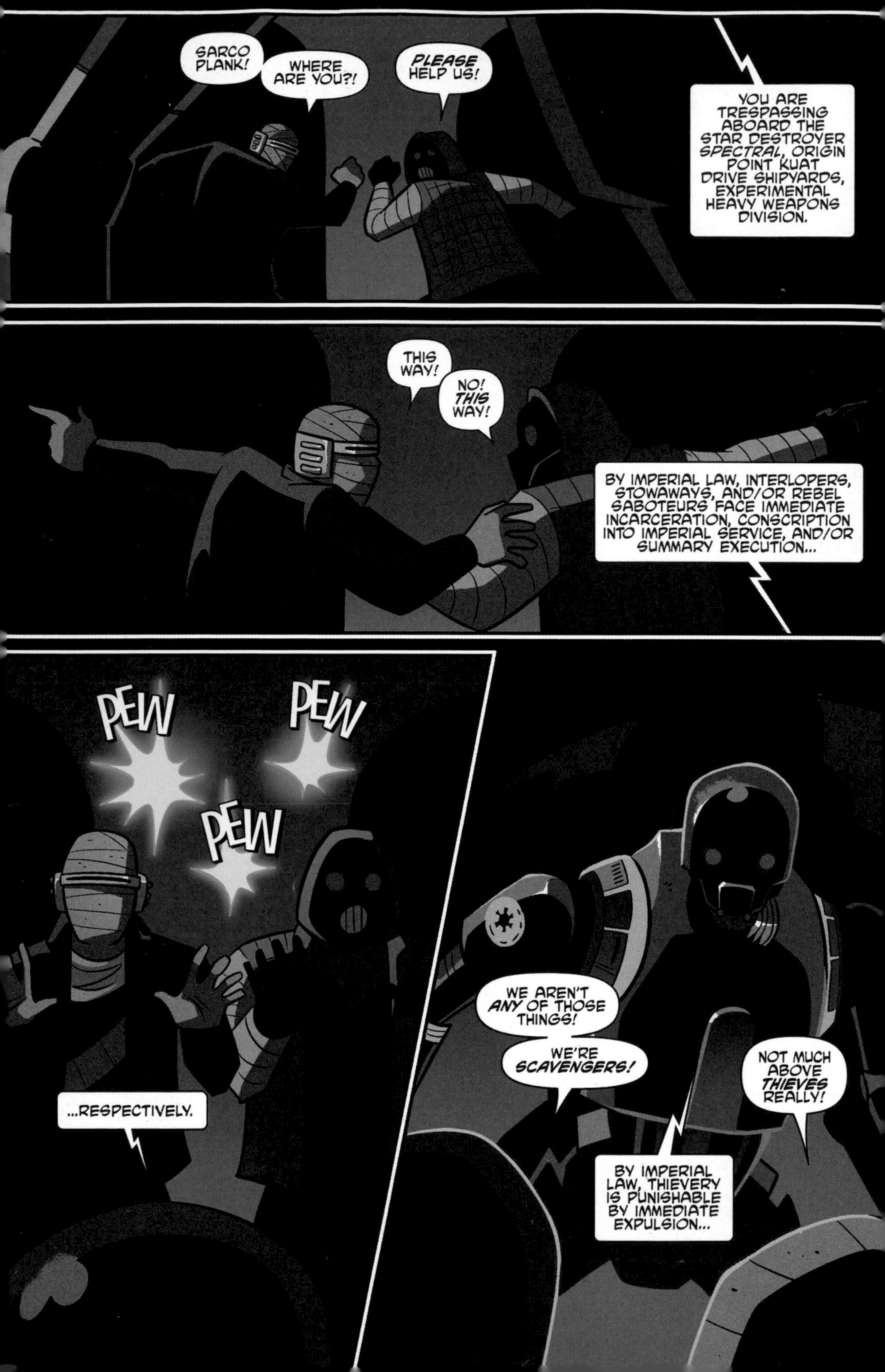
SARCO PLANK!
WHERE ARE YOU?!
PLEASE HELP US!
YOU ARE TRESPASSING ABOARD THE STAR DESTROYER SPECTRAL, ORIGIN POINT KUAT DRIVE SHIPYARDS, EXPERIMENTAL HEAVY WEAPONS DIVISION.
THIS WAY!
NO! THIS WAY!
BY IMPERIAL LAW, INTERLOPERS, STOWAWAYS, AND/OR REBEL SABOTEURS FACE IMMEDIATE INCARCERATION, CONSCRIPTION INTO IMPERIAL SERVICE, AND/OR SUMMARY EXECUTION...
PEW
PEW
PEW
...RESPECTIVELY.
WE AREN'T ANY OF THOSE THINGS!
WE'RE SCAVENGERS!
NOT MUCH ABOVE THIEVES REALLY!
BY IMPERIAL LAW, THIEVERY IS PUNISHABLE BY IMMEDIATE EXPULSION...

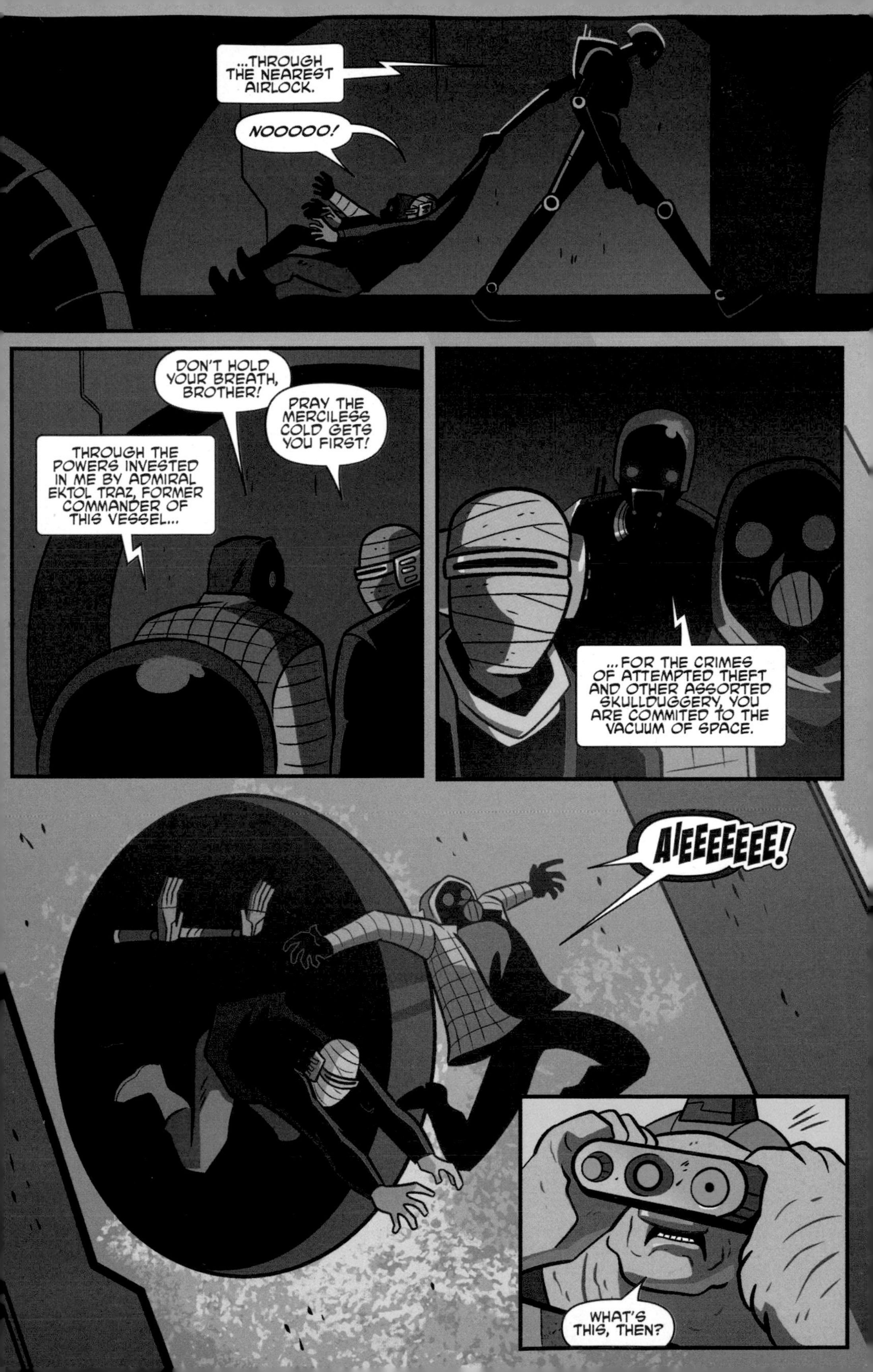
...THROUGH THE NEAREST AIRLOCK.
NOOOOO!
THROUGH THE POWERS INVESTED IN ME BY ADMIRAL EKTOL TRAZ, FORMER COMMANDER OF THIS VESSEL...
DON'T HOLD YOUR BREATH, BROTHER!
PRAY THE MERCILESS COLD GETS YOU FIRST!
...FOR THE CRIMES OF ATTEMPTED THEFT AND OTHER ASSORTED SKULLDUGGERY, YOU ARE COMMITED TO THE VACUUM OF SPACE.
AIEEEEEEE!
WHAT'S THIS, THEN?

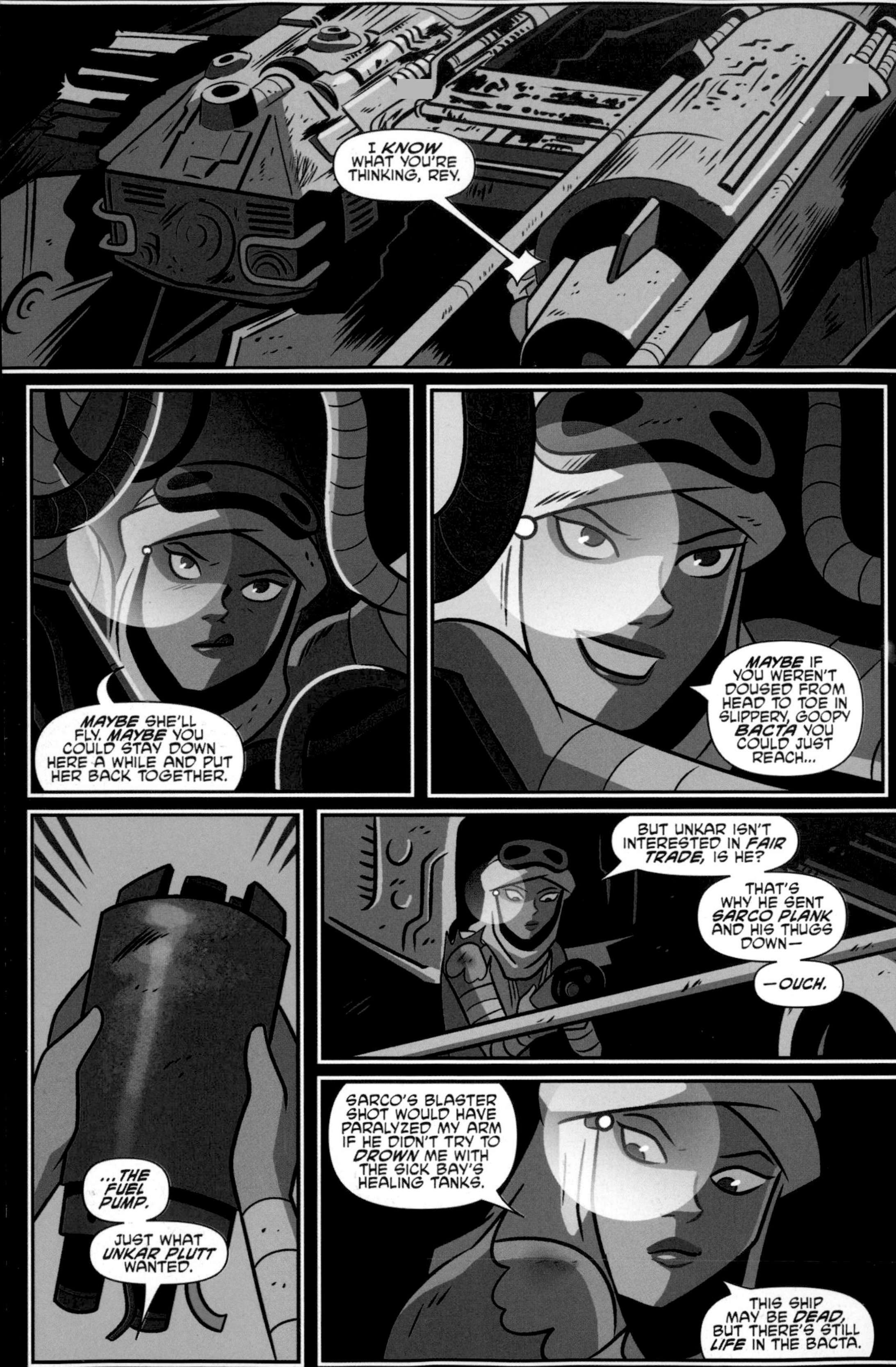
I KNOW WHAT YOU'RE THINKING, REY.
MAYBE SHE'LL FLY. MAYBE YOU COULD STAY DOWN HERE A WHILE AND PUT HER BACK TOGETHER.
MAYBE IF YOU WEREN'T DOUSED FROM HEAD TO TOE IN SLIPPERY, GOOPY BACTA YOU COULD JUST REACH...
...THE FUEL PUMP.
JUST WHAT UNKAR PLUTT WANTED.
BUT UNKAR ISN'T INTERESTED IN FAIR TRADE, IS HE?
THAT'S WHY HE SENT SARCO PLANK AND HIS THUGS DOWN—
—OUCH.
SARCO'S BLASTER SHOT WOULD HAVE PARALYZED MY ARM IF HE DIDN'T TRY TO DROWN ME WITH THE SICK BAY'S HEALING TANKS.
THIS SHIP MAY BE DEAD, BUT THERE'S STILL LIFE IN THE BACTA.

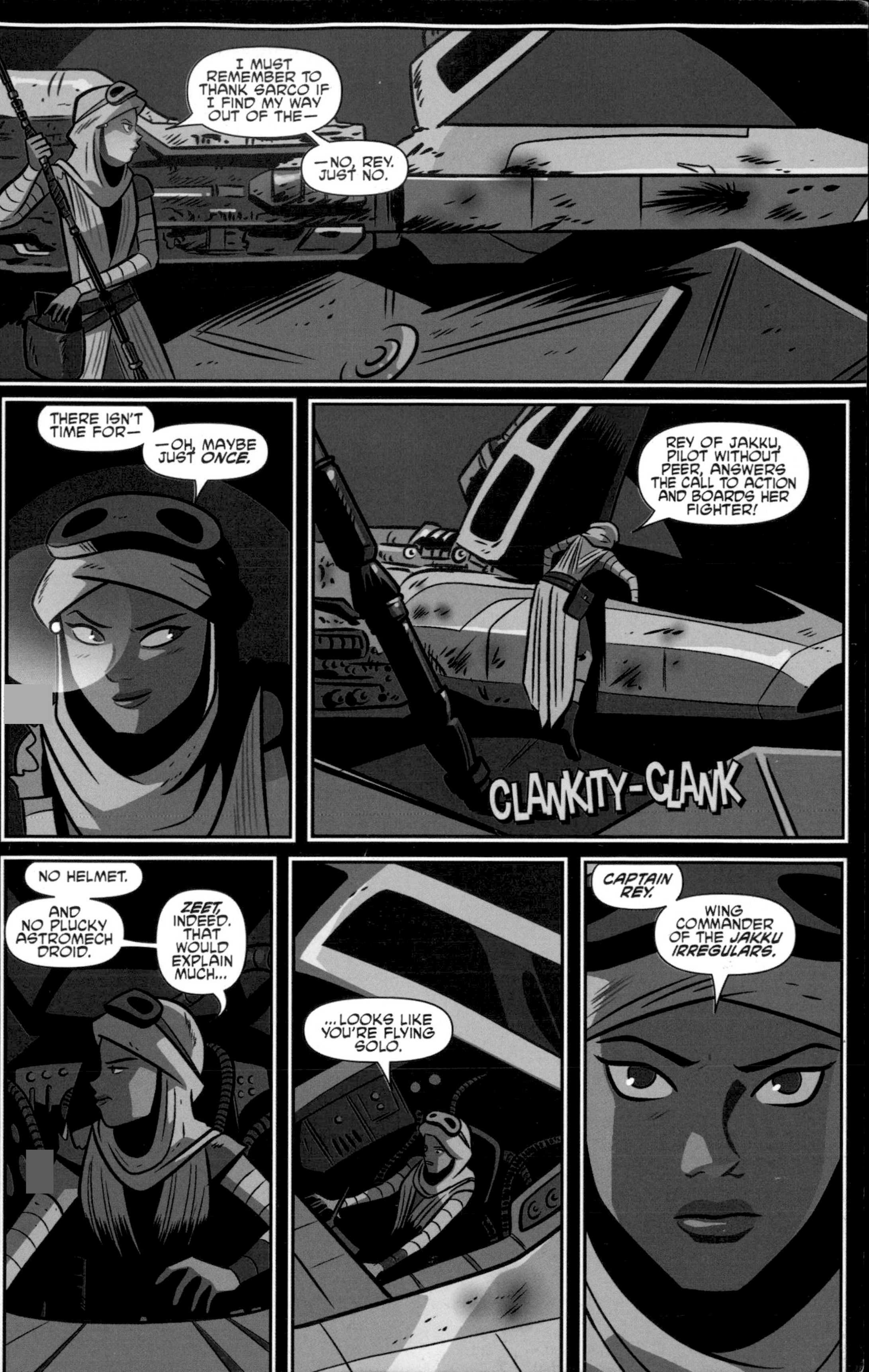
I MUST REMEMBER TO THANK SARCO IF I FIND MY WAY OUT OF THE—
—NO, REY. JUST NO.
THERE ISN'T TIME FOR—
—OH, MAYBE JUST *ONCE.*
REY OF JAKKU, PILOT WITHOUT PEER, ANSWERS THE CALL TO ACTION AND BOARDS HER FIGHTER!
CLANKITY-CLANK
NO HELMET.
AND NO PLUCKY ASTROMECH DROID.
ZEET, INDEED. THAT WOULD EXPLAIN MUCH...
...LOOKS LIKE YOU'RE FLYING SOLO.
CAPTAIN REY.
WING COMMANDER OF THE *JAKKU IRREGULARS.*

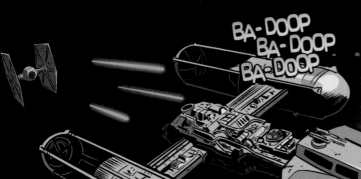

BA-DOOP BA-DOOP BA-DOOP

HUSH NOW, ZEET!

IT'S ONLY CHUNKS OF ICE AND VERY SMALL ROCKS!

NOW LET ME CONCENTRATE ON *FLYING*.

I'VE GOT THIS.

SKREEEEEE

BEEP BOOP BOP

ALL RIGHT, SO NOT ALL OF THE ROCKS ARE *SMALL*.

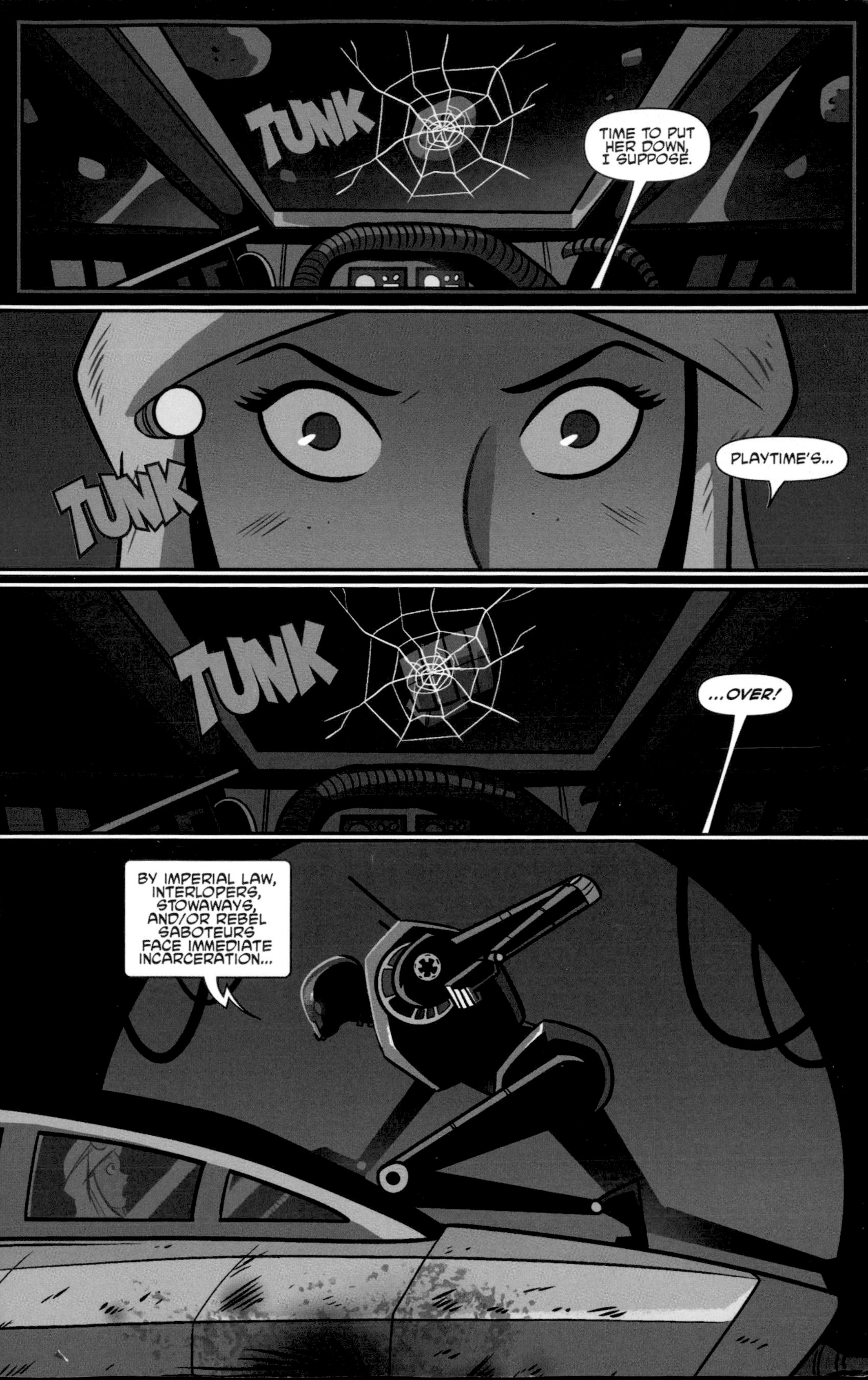
TUNK
TIME TO PUT HER DOWN, I SUPPOSE.
TUNK
PLAYTIME'S...
TUNK
...OVER!
BY IMPERIAL LAW, INTERLOPERS, STOWAWAYS, AND/OR REBEL SABOTEURS FACE IMMEDIATE INCARCERATION...

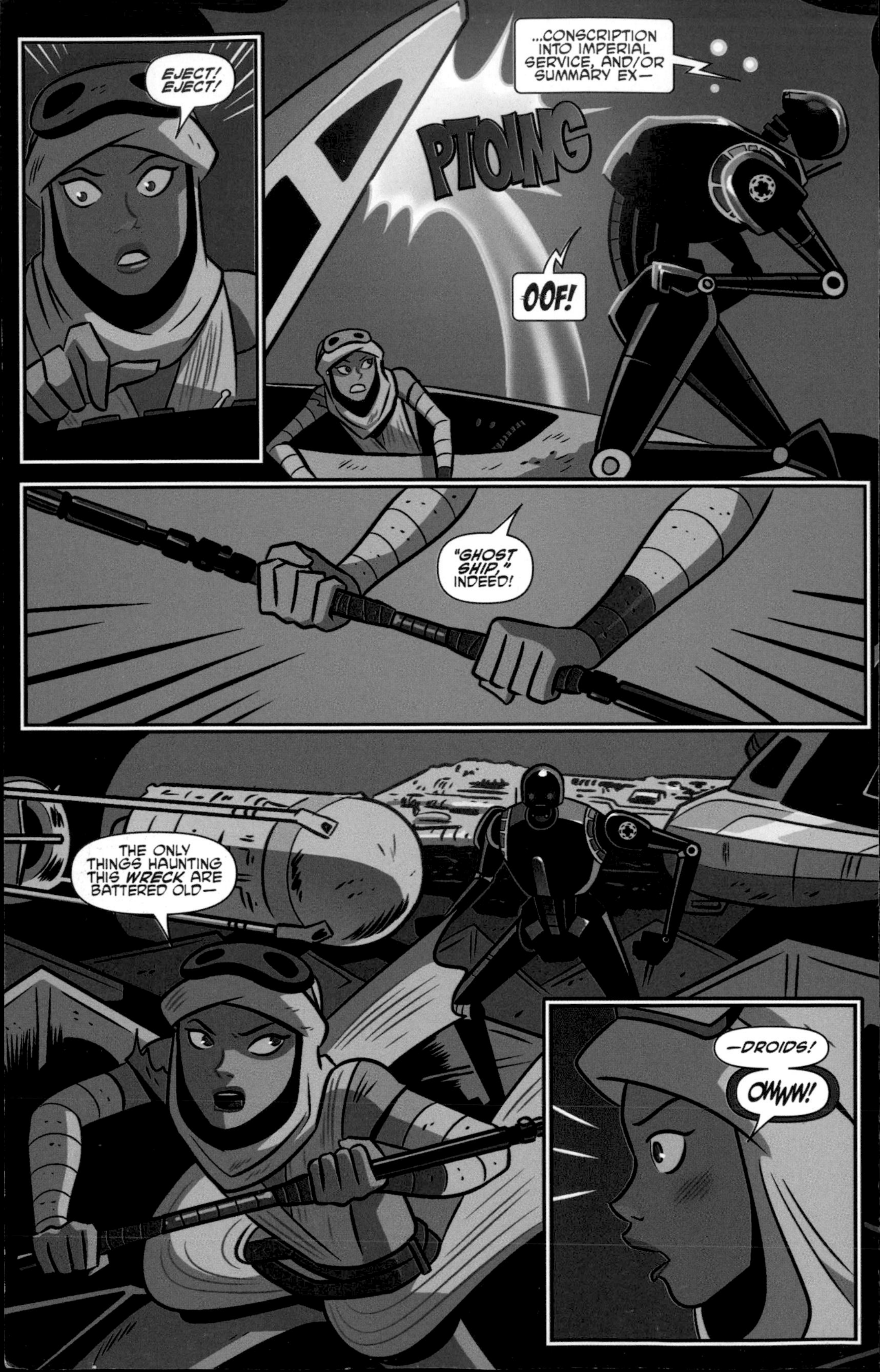
EJECT! EJECT!
...CONSCRIPTION INTO IMPERIAL SERVICE, AND/OR SUMMARY EX—
PTOING
OOF!
"GHOST SHIP," INDEED!
THE ONLY THINGS HAUNTING THIS WRECK ARE BATTERED OLD—
—DROIDS!
OWWW!

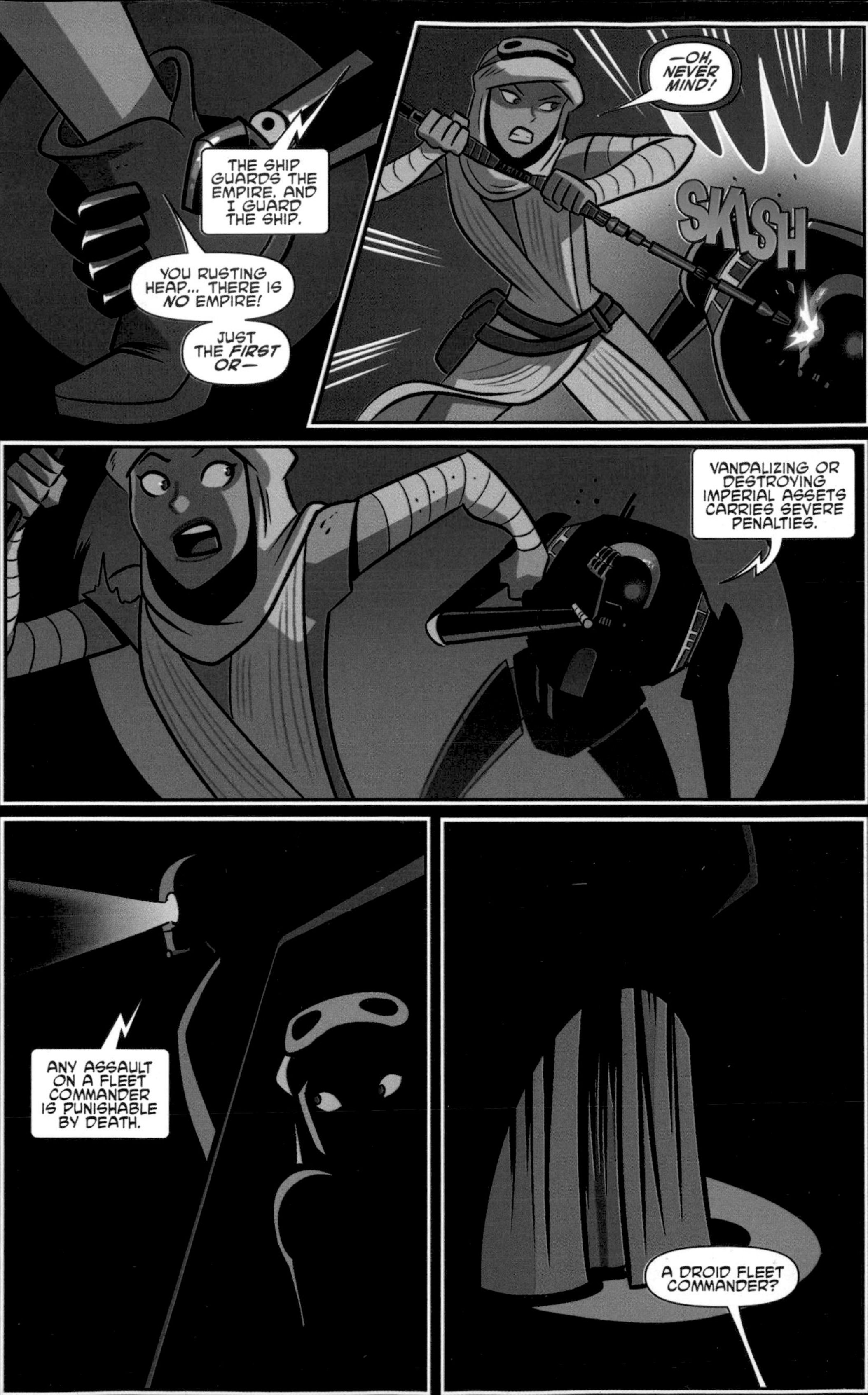
THE SHIP GUARDS THE EMPIRE. AND I GUARD THE SHIP.
YOU RUSTING HEAP... THERE IS NO EMPIRE!
JUST THE FIRST OR—
—OH, NEVER MIND!
SKISH
VANDALIZING OR DESTROYING IMPERIAL ASSETS CARRIES SEVERE PENALTIES.
ANY ASSAULT ON A FLEET COMMANDER IS PUNISHABLE BY DEATH.
A DROID FLEET COMMANDER?

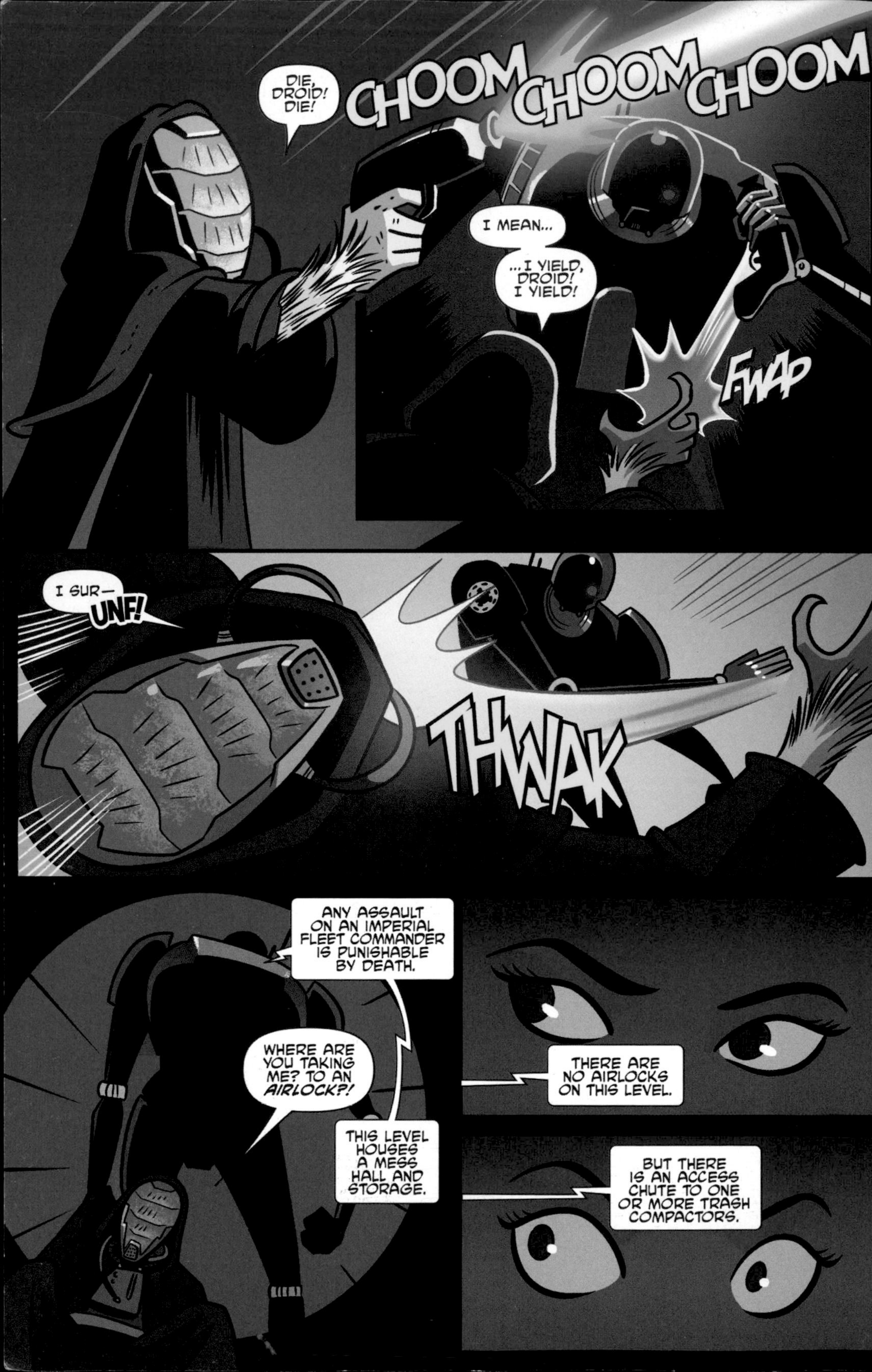

DIE, DROID! DIE!
CHOOM CHOOM CHOOM
I MEAN...
...I YIELD, DROID! I YIELD!
FWAP
I SUR—
UNF!
THWAK
ANY ASSAULT ON AN IMPERIAL FLEET COMMANDER IS PUNISHABLE BY DEATH.
WHERE ARE YOU TAKING ME? TO AN *AIRLOCK?!*
THIS LEVEL HOUSES A MESS HALL AND STORAGE.
THERE ARE NO AIRLOCKS ON THIS LEVEL.
BUT THERE IS AN ACCESS CHUTE TO ONE OR MORE TRASH COMPACTORS.

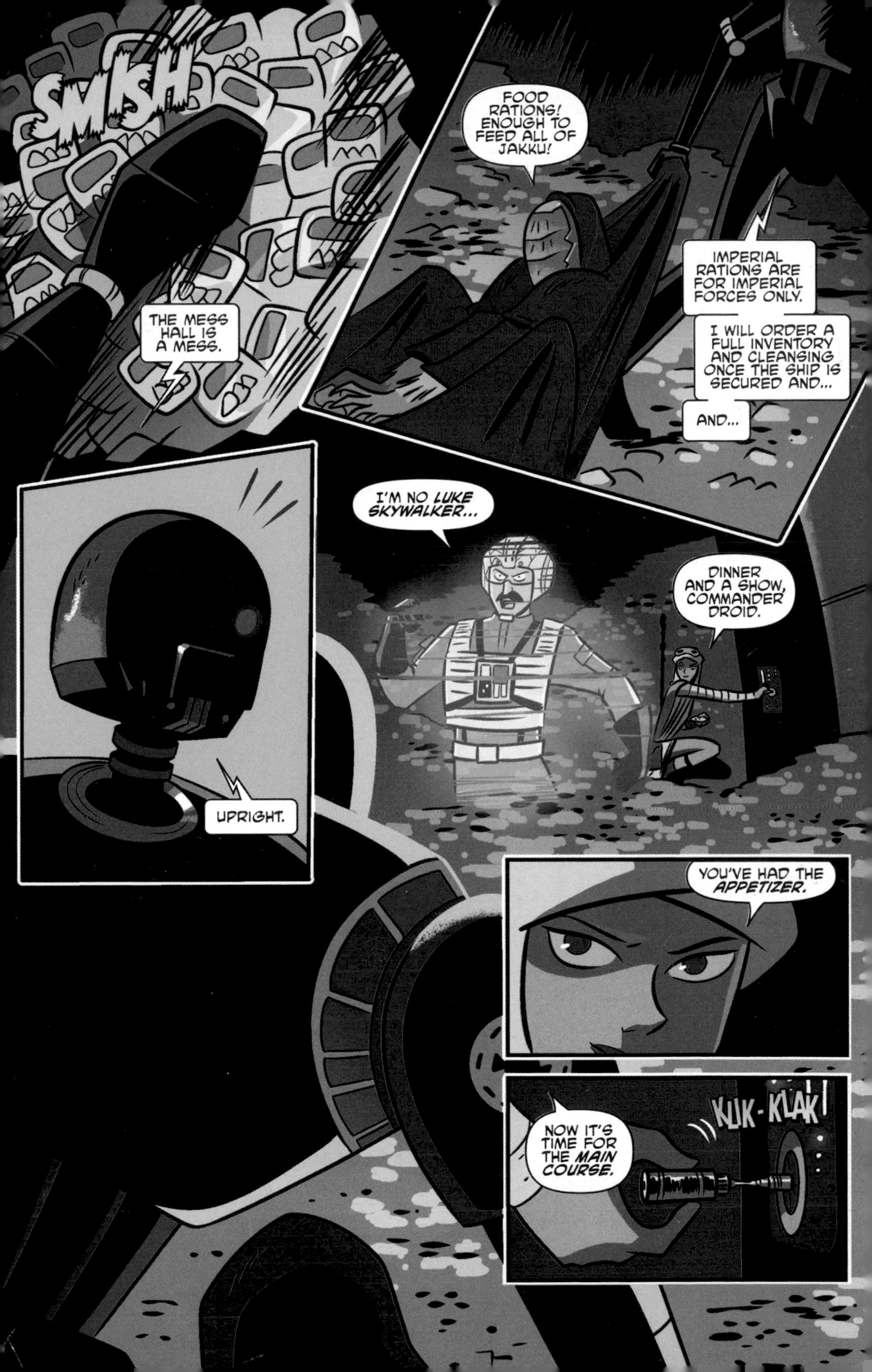
SMISH
THE MESS HALL IS A MESS.
FOOD RATIONS! ENOUGH TO FEED ALL OF JAKKU!
IMPERIAL RATIONS ARE FOR IMPERIAL FORCES ONLY.
I WILL ORDER A FULL INVENTORY AND CLEANSING ONCE THE SHIP IS SECURED AND...
AND...
UPRIGHT.
I'M NO LUKE SKYWALKER...
DINNER AND A SHOW, COMMANDER DROID.
YOU'VE HAD THE APPETIZER.
NOW IT'S TIME FOR THE MAIN COURSE.
KLIK-KLAK!

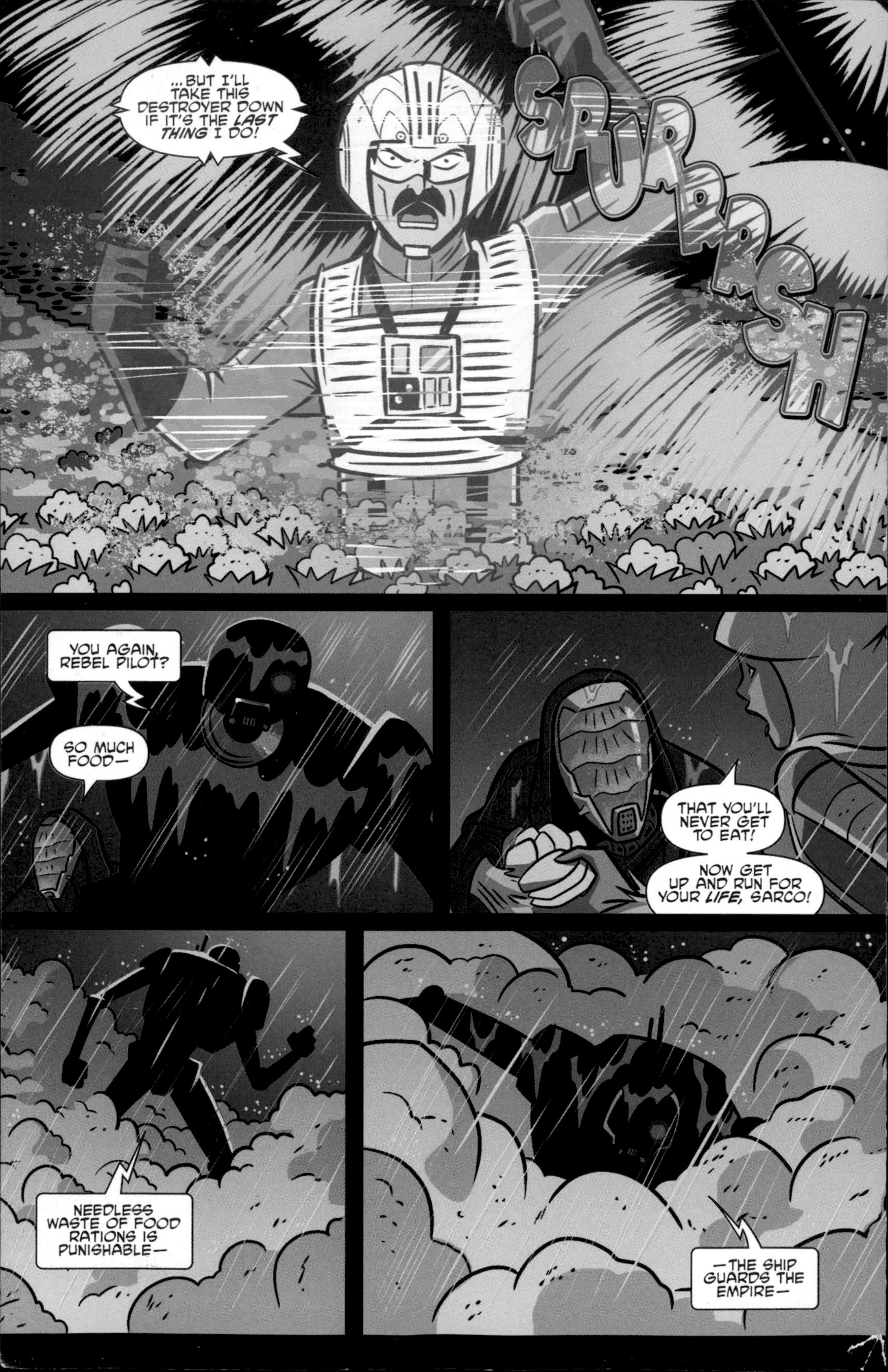
...BUT I'LL TAKE THIS DESTROYER DOWN IF IT'S THE *LAST THING* I DO!
SPRURRRSH
YOU AGAIN, REBEL PILOT?
SO MUCH FOOD—
THAT YOU'LL NEVER GET TO EAT!
NOW GET UP AND RUN FOR YOUR *LIFE*, SARCO!
NEEDLESS WASTE OF FOOD RATIONS IS PUNISHABLE—
—THE SHIP GUARDS THE EMPIRE—

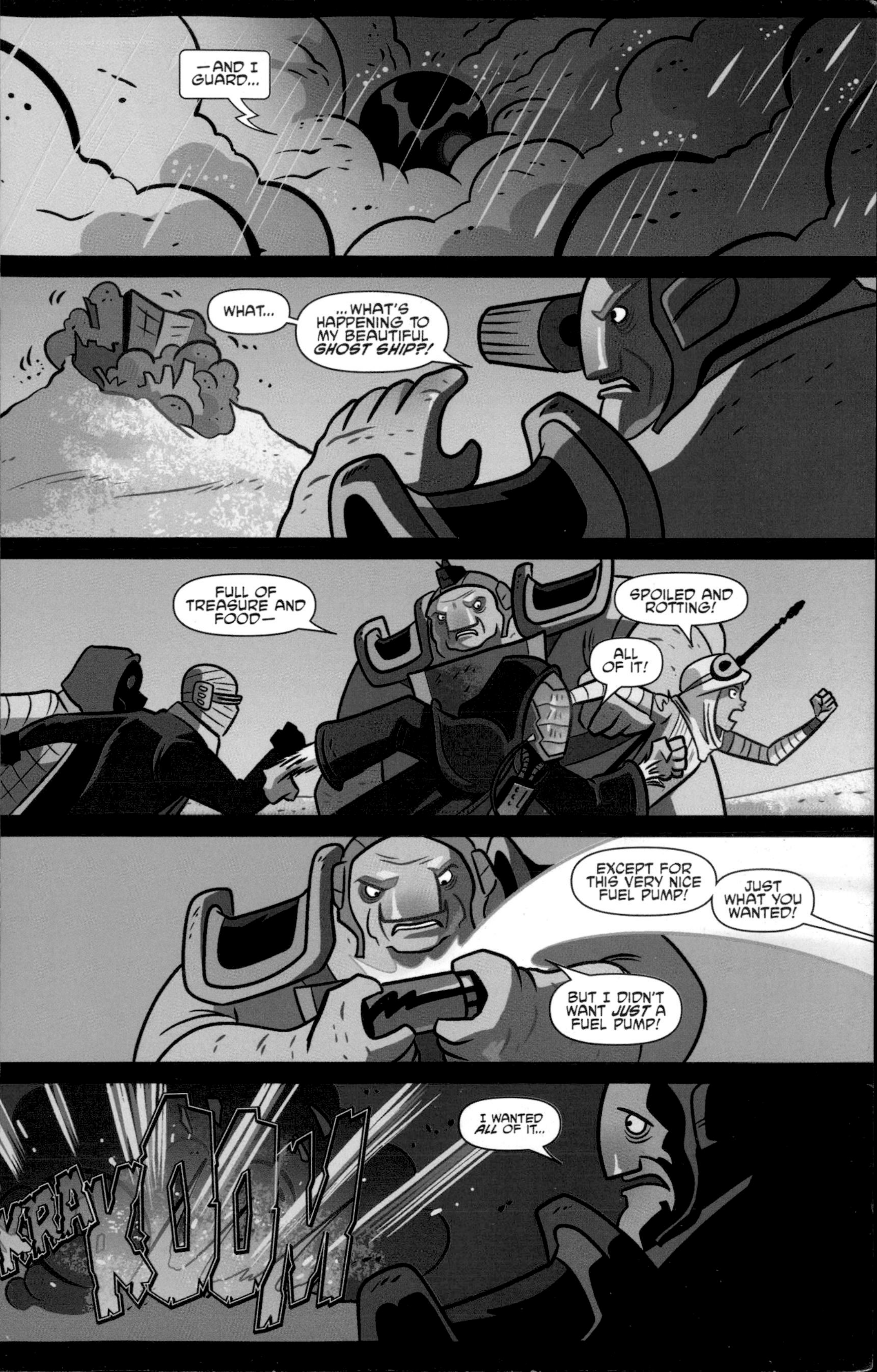
—AND I GUARD...
WHAT...
...WHAT'S HAPPENING TO MY BEAUTIFUL *GHOST SHIP?!*
FULL OF TREASURE AND FOOD—
SPOILED AND ROTTING!
ALL OF IT!
EXCEPT FOR THIS VERY NICE FUEL PUMP!
JUST WHAT YOU WANTED!
BUT I DIDN'T WANT *JUST* A FUEL PUMP!
I WANTED *ALL* OF IT...
KRAKOOM

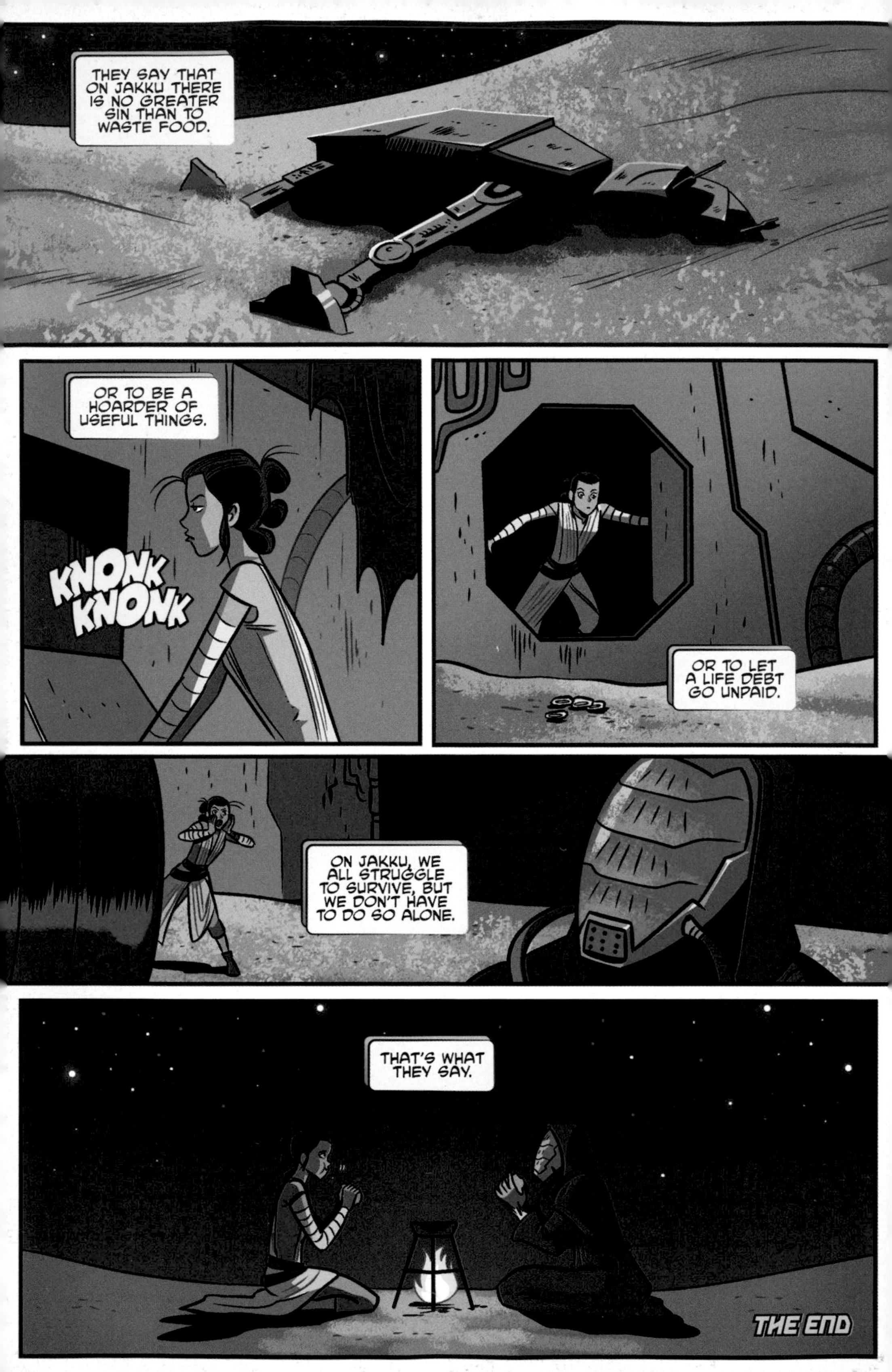
THEY SAY THAT ON JAKKU THERE IS NO GREATER SIN THAN TO WASTE FOOD.
OR TO BE A HOARDER OF USEFUL THINGS.
KNONK KNONK
OR TO LET A LIFE DEBT GO UNPAID.
ON JAKKU, WE ALL STRUGGLE TO SURVIVE, BUT WE DON'T HAVE TO DO SO ALONE.
THAT'S WHAT THEY SAY.
THE END

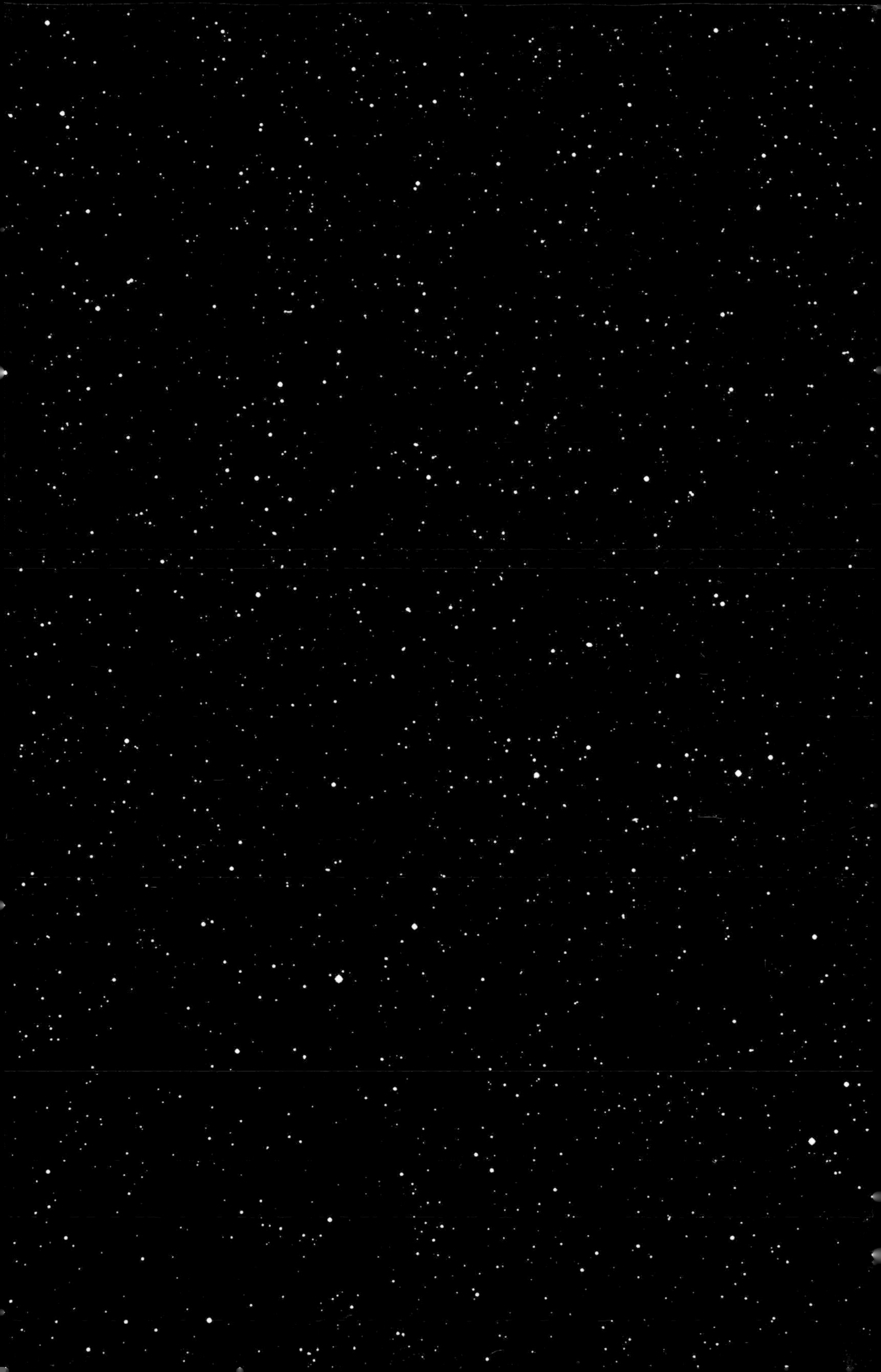

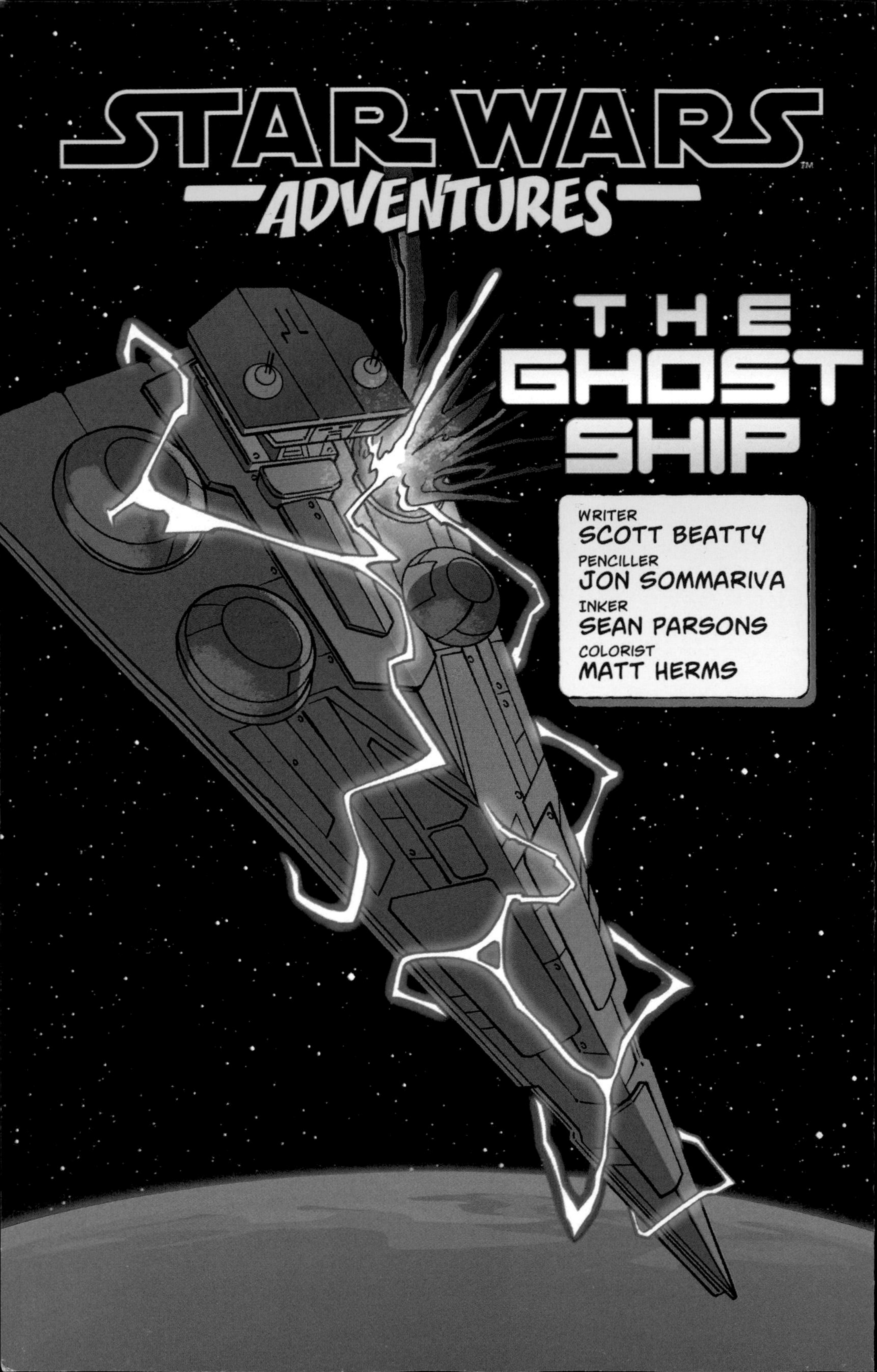
STAR WARS™
ADVENTURES
THE GHOST SHIP
WRITER
SCOTT BEATTY
PENCILLER
JON SOMMARIVA
INKER
SEAN PARSONS
COLORIST
MATT HERMS

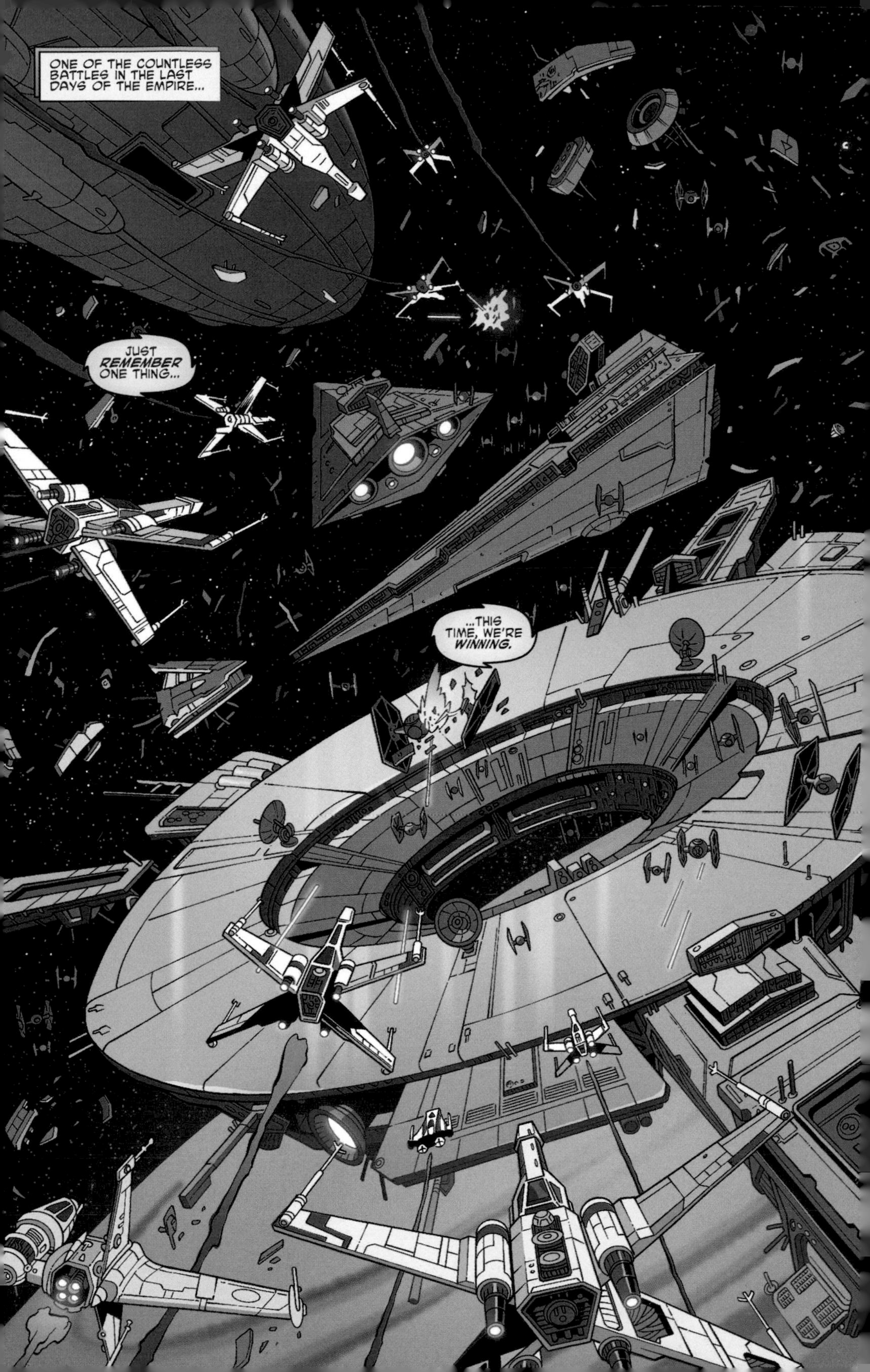
ONE OF THE COUNTLESS BATTLES IN THE LAST DAYS OF THE EMPIRE...
JUST REMEMBER ONE THING...
...THIS TIME, WE'RE WINNING.

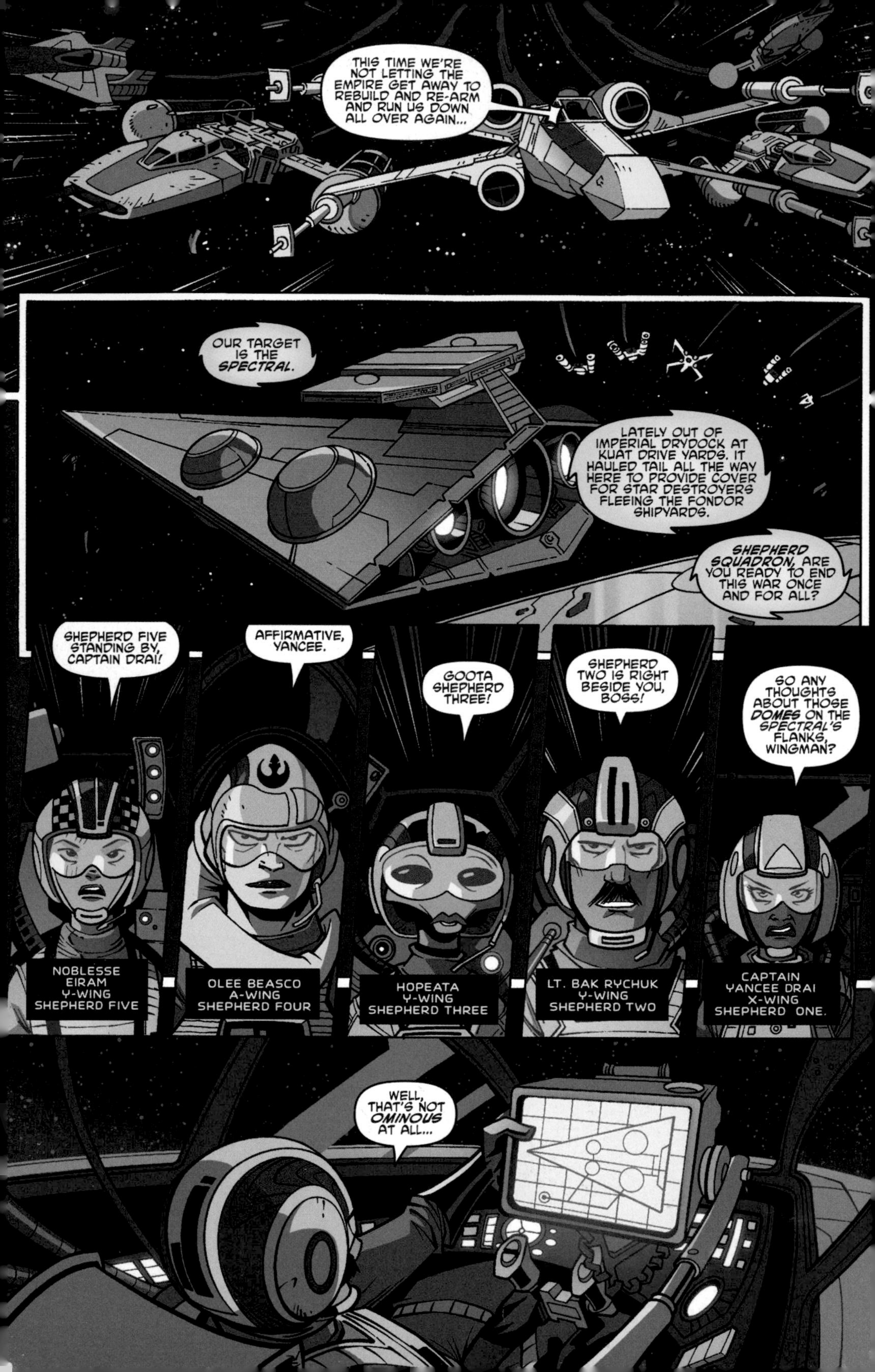
THIS TIME WE'RE NOT LETTING THE EMPIRE GET AWAY TO REBUILD AND RE-ARM AND RUN US DOWN ALL OVER AGAIN...
OUR TARGET IS THE *SPECTRAL*.
LATELY OUT OF IMPERIAL DRYDOCK AT KUAT DRIVE YARDS. IT HAULED TAIL ALL THE WAY HERE TO PROVIDE COVER FOR STAR DESTROYERS FLEEING THE FONDOR SHIPYARDS.
SHEPHERD SQUADRON, ARE YOU READY TO END THIS WAR ONCE AND FOR ALL?
SHEPHERD FIVE STANDING BY, CAPTAIN DRAI!
NOBLESSE EIRAM Y-WING SHEPHERD FIVE
AFFIRMATIVE, YANCEE.
OLEE BEASCO A-WING SHEPHERD FOUR
GOOTA SHEPHERD THREE!
HOPEATA Y-WING SHEPHERD THREE
SHEPHERD TWO IS RIGHT BESIDE YOU, BOSS!
LT. BAK RYCHUK Y-WING SHEPHERD TWO
SO ANY THOUGHTS ABOUT THOSE *DOMES* ON THE *SPECTRAL'S* FLANKS, WINGMAN?
CAPTAIN YANCEE DRAI X-WING SHEPHERD ONE.
WELL, THAT'S NOT *OMINOUS* AT ALL...

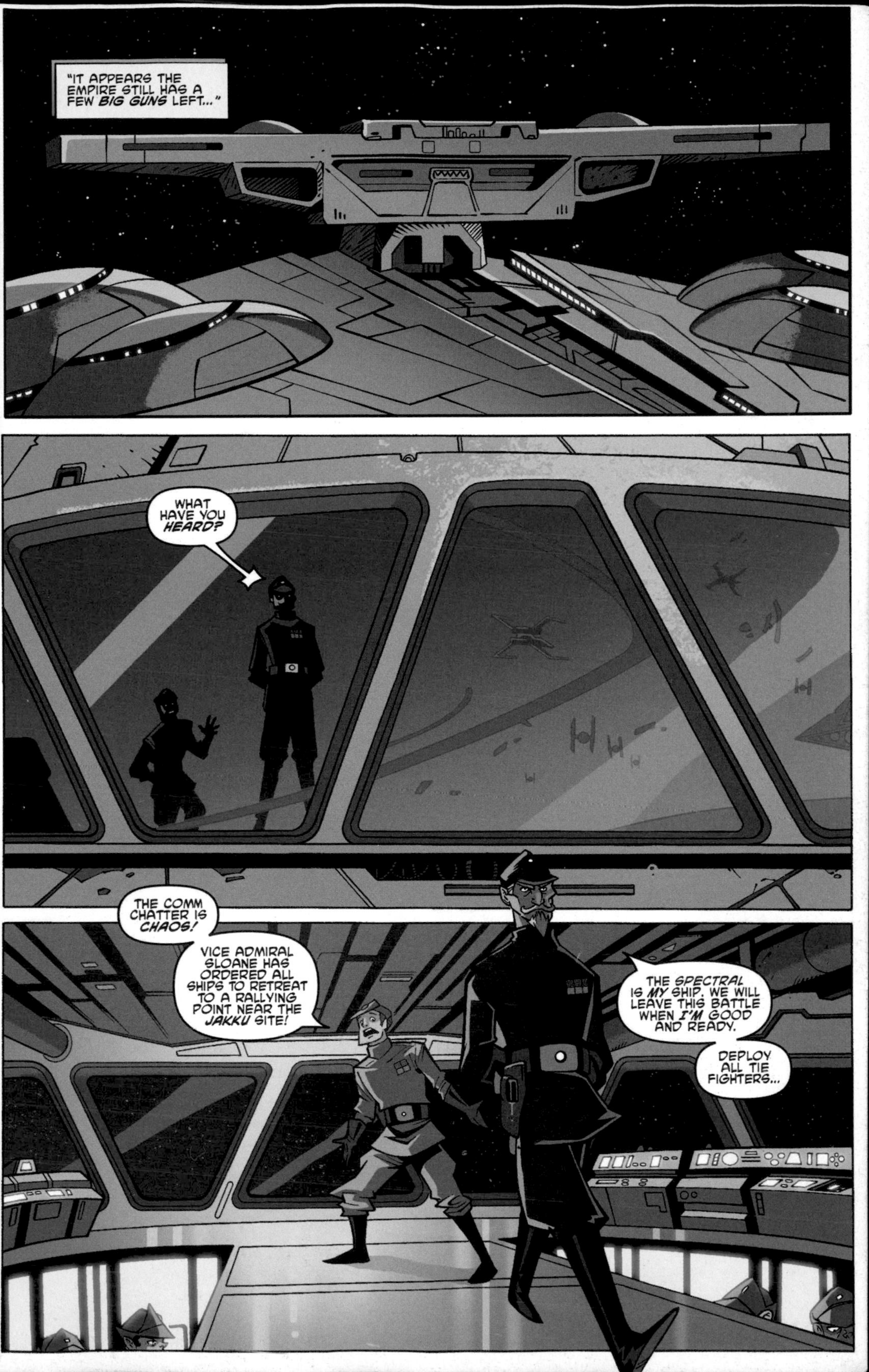
"IT APPEARS THE EMPIRE STILL HAS A FEW BIG GUNS LEFT..."
WHAT HAVE YOU HEARD?
THE COMM CHATTER IS CHAOS!
VICE ADMIRAL SLOANE HAS ORDERED ALL SHIPS TO RETREAT TO A RALLYING POINT NEAR THE JAKKU SITE!
THE SPECTRAL IS MY SHIP. WE WILL LEAVE THIS BATTLE WHEN I'M GOOD AND READY.
DEPLOY ALL TIE FIGHTERS...

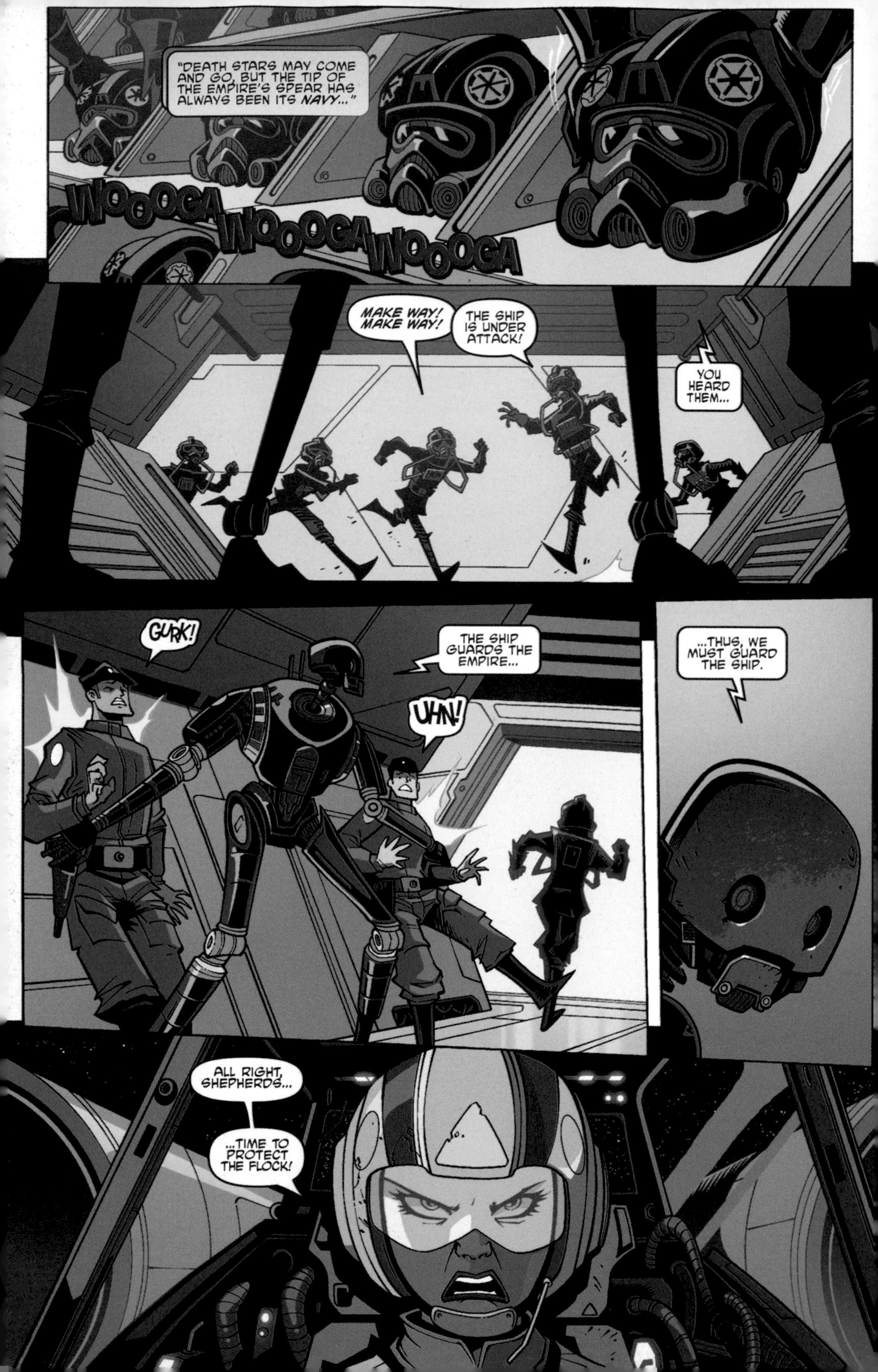
"DEATH STARS MAY COME AND GO, BUT THE TIP OF THE EMPIRE'S SPEAR HAS ALWAYS BEEN ITS *NAVY*..."
WOOOGA WOOOGA WOOOGA
MAKE WAY! MAKE WAY!
THE SHIP IS UNDER ATTACK!
YOU HEARD THEM...
GURK!
THE SHIP GUARDS THE EMPIRE...
UHN!
...THUS, WE MUST GUARD THE SHIP.
ALL RIGHT, SHEPHERDS...
...TIME TO PROTECT THE FLOCK!

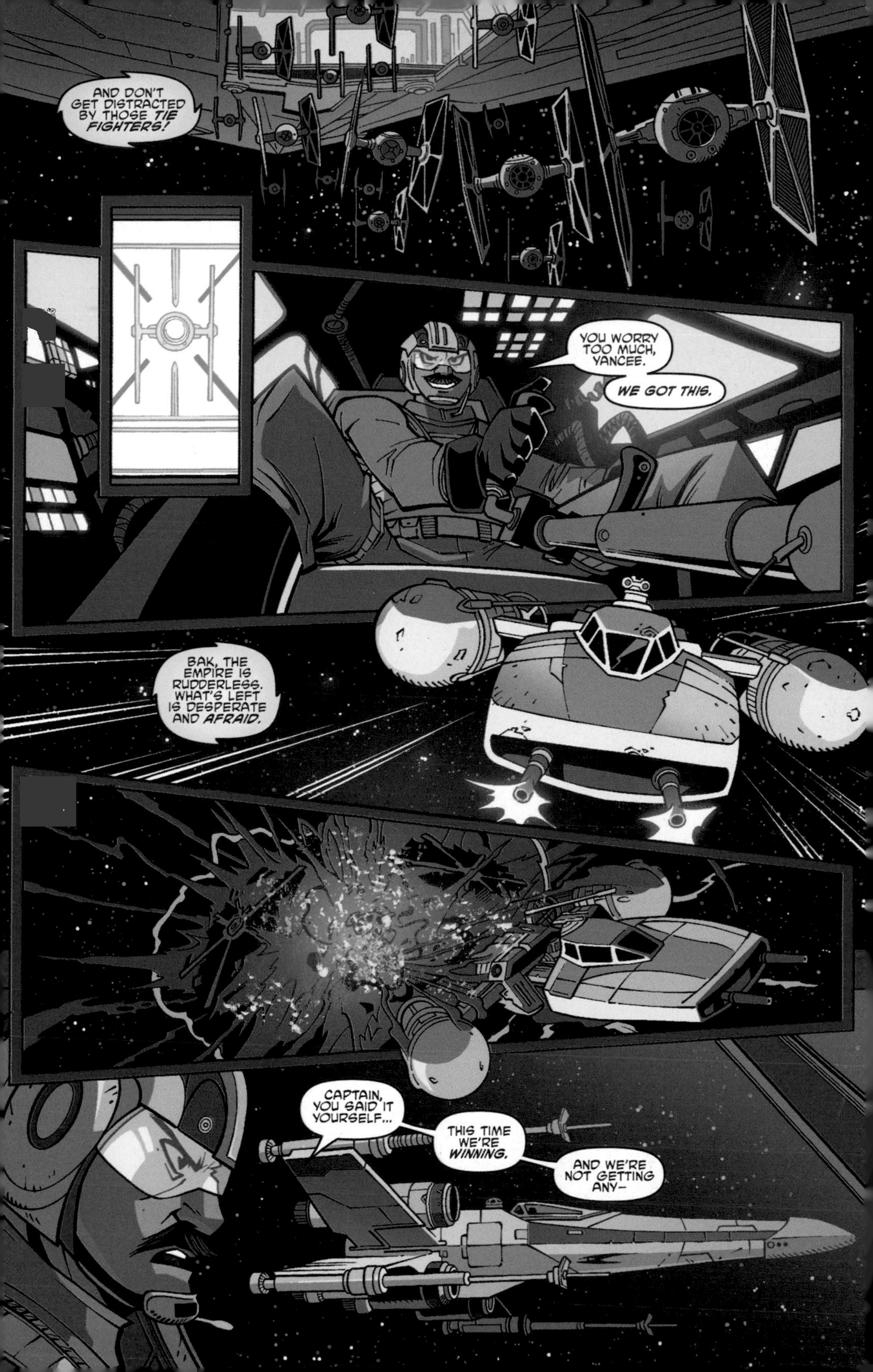
AND DON'T GET DISTRACTED BY THOSE *TIE FIGHTERS!*
YOU WORRY TOO MUCH, YANCEE.
WE GOT THIS.
BAK, THE EMPIRE IS RUDDERLESS. WHAT'S LEFT IS DESPERATE AND *AFRAID.*
CAPTAIN, YOU SAID IT YOURSELF...
THIS TIME WE'RE *WINNING.*
AND WE'RE NOT GETTING ANY—

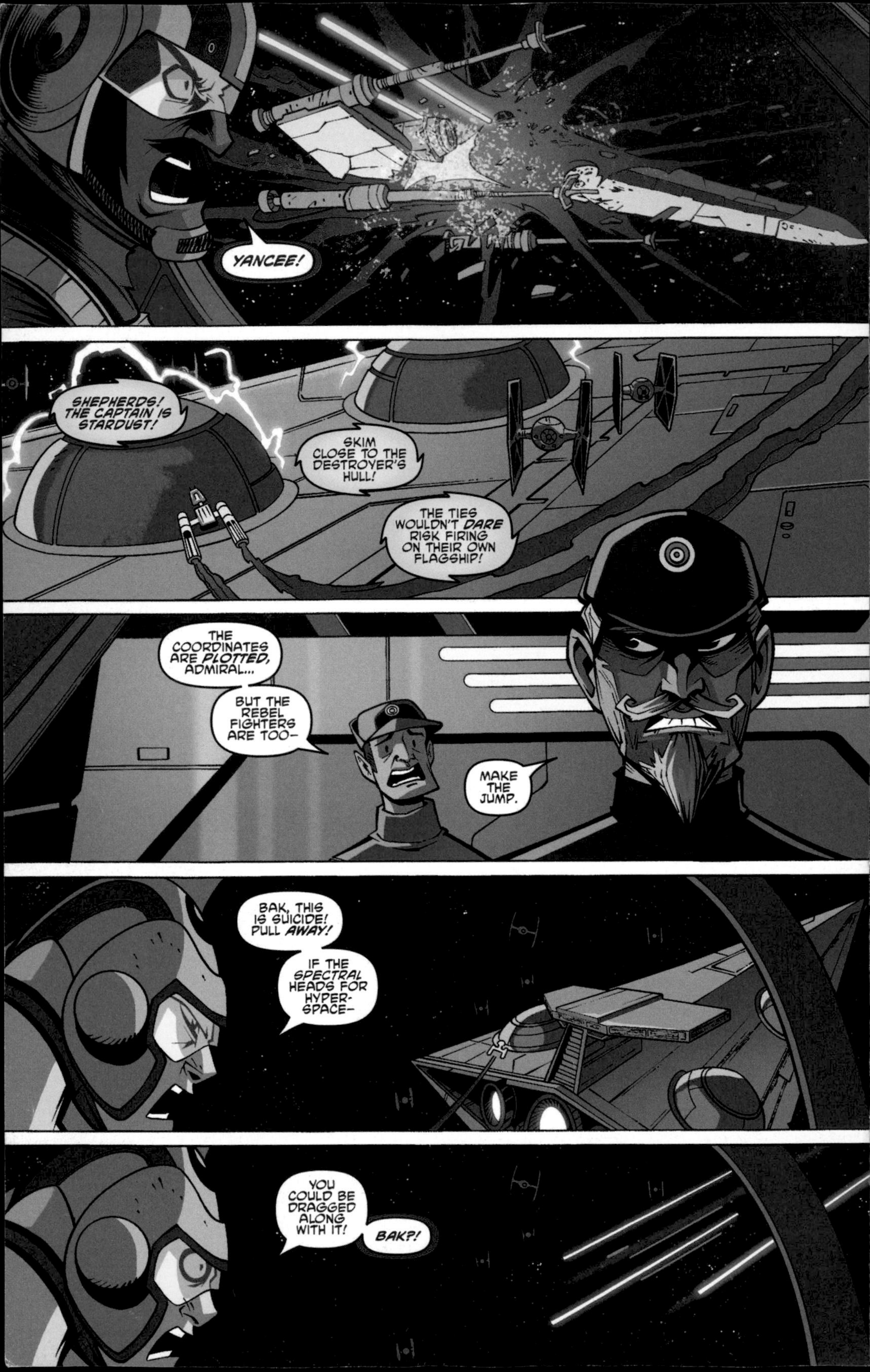
YANCEE!
SHEPHERDS! THE CAPTAIN IS STARDUST!
SKIM CLOSE TO THE DESTROYER'S HULL!
THE TIES WOULDN'T DARE RISK FIRING ON THEIR OWN FLAGSHIP!
THE COORDINATES ARE PLOTTED, ADMIRAL...
BUT THE REBEL FIGHTERS ARE TOO-
MAKE THE JUMP.
BAK, THIS IS SUICIDE! PULL AWAY!
IF THE SPECTRAL HEADS FOR HYPER-SPACE-
YOU COULD BE DRAGGED ALONG WITH IT!
BAK?!

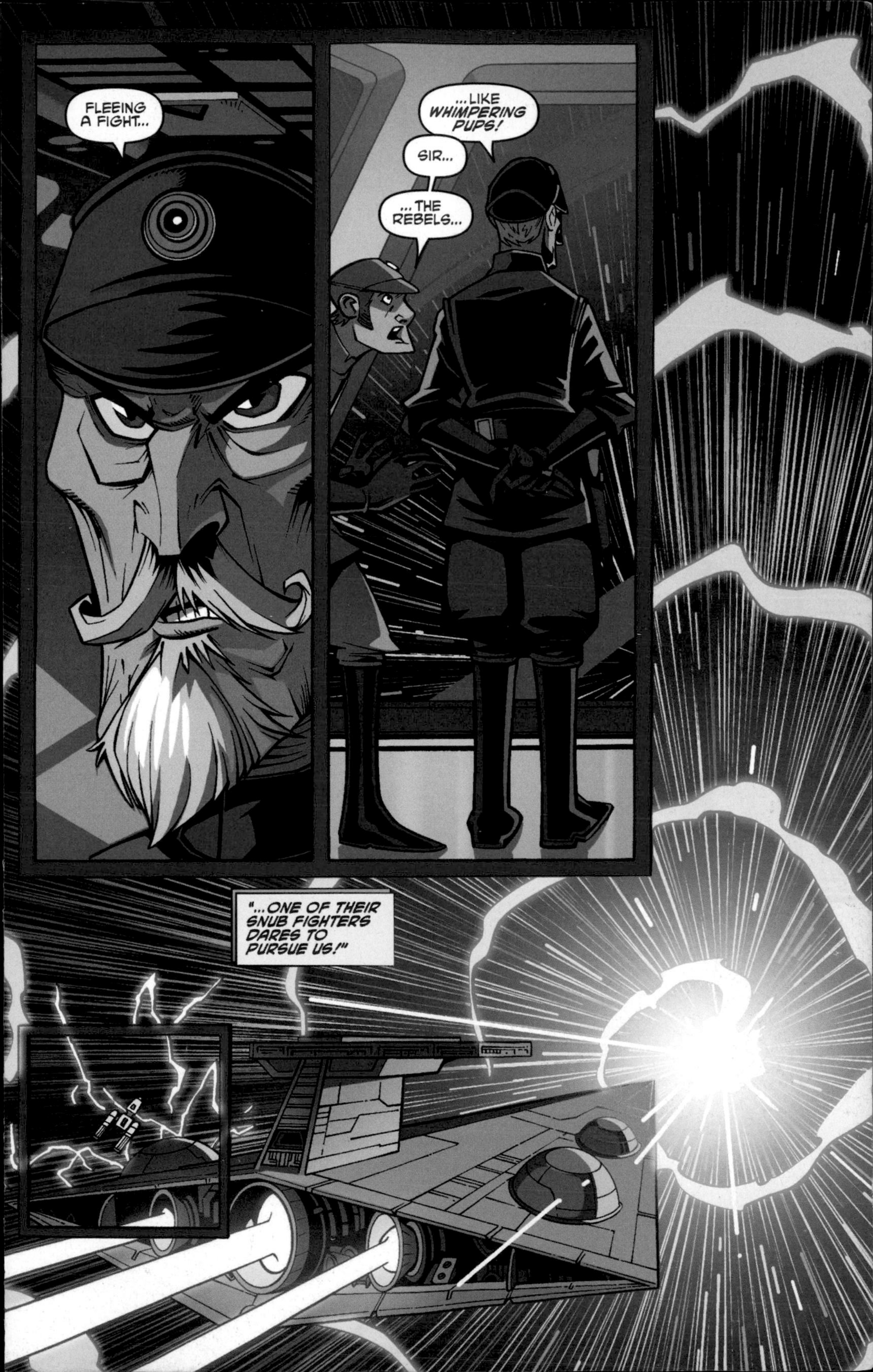
FLEEING A FIGHT...
...LIKE WHIMPERING PUPS!
SIR...
...THE REBELS...
"...ONE OF THEIR SNUB FIGHTERS DARES TO PURSUE US!"

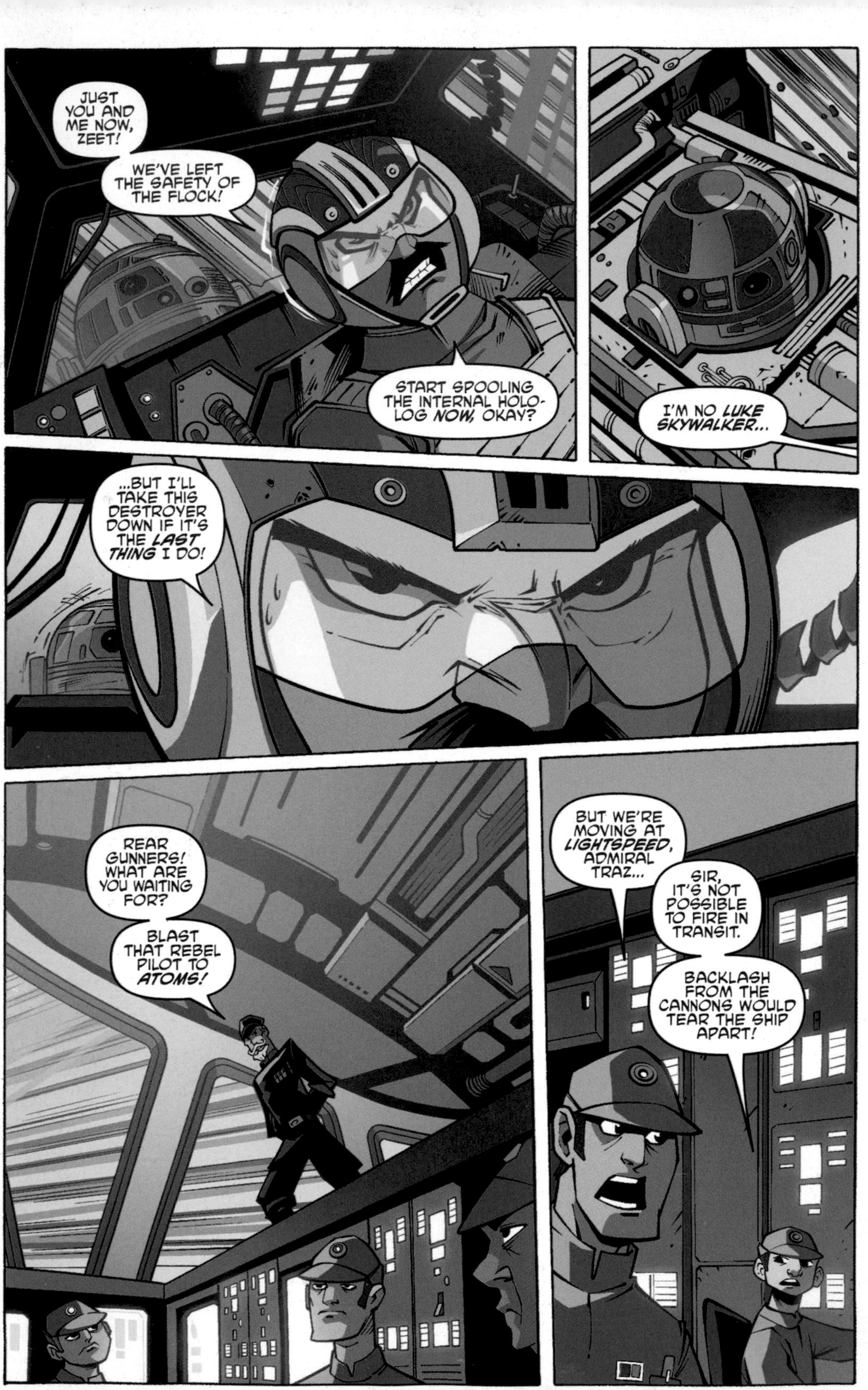
JUST YOU AND ME NOW, ZEET!
WE'VE LEFT THE SAFETY OF THE FLOCK!
START SPOOLING THE INTERNAL HOLO-LOG NOW, OKAY?
I'M NO LUKE SKYWALKER...
...BUT I'LL TAKE THIS DESTROYER DOWN IF IT'S THE LAST THING I DO!
REAR GUNNERS! WHAT ARE YOU WAITING FOR?
BLAST THAT REBEL PILOT TO ATOMS!
BUT WE'RE MOVING AT LIGHTSPEED, ADMIRAL TRAZ...
SIR, IT'S NOT POSSIBLE TO FIRE IN TRANSIT.
BACKLASH FROM THE CANNONS WOULD TEAR THE SHIP APART!

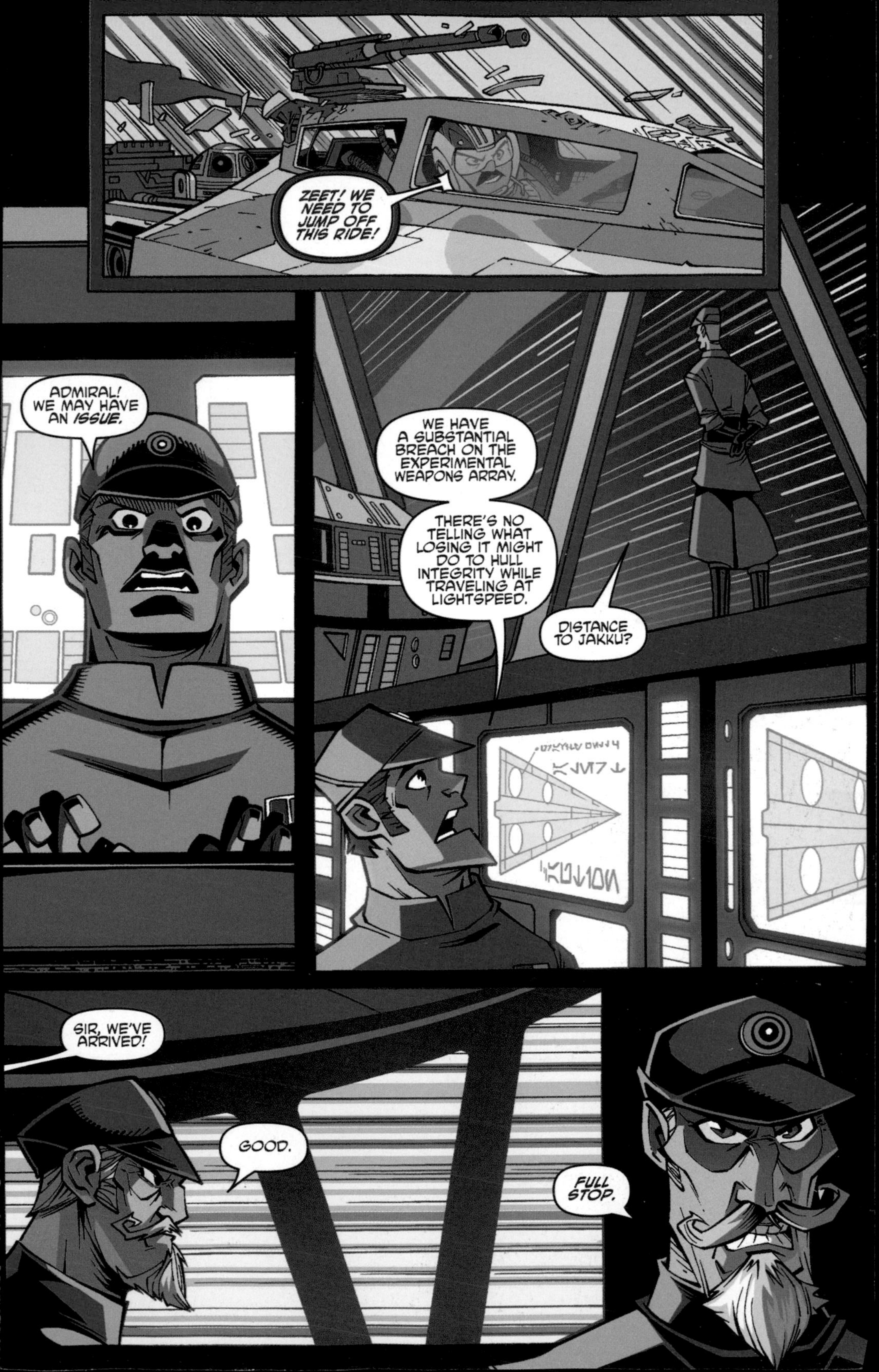
ZEET! WE NEED TO JUMP OFF THIS RIDE!
ADMIRAL! WE MAY HAVE AN ISSUE.
WE HAVE A SUBSTANTIAL BREACH ON THE EXPERIMENTAL WEAPONS ARRAY.
THERE'S NO TELLING WHAT LOSING IT MIGHT DO TO HULL INTEGRITY WHILE TRAVELING AT LIGHTSPEED.
DISTANCE TO JAKKU?
SIR, WE'VE ARRIVED!
GOOD.
FULL STOP.

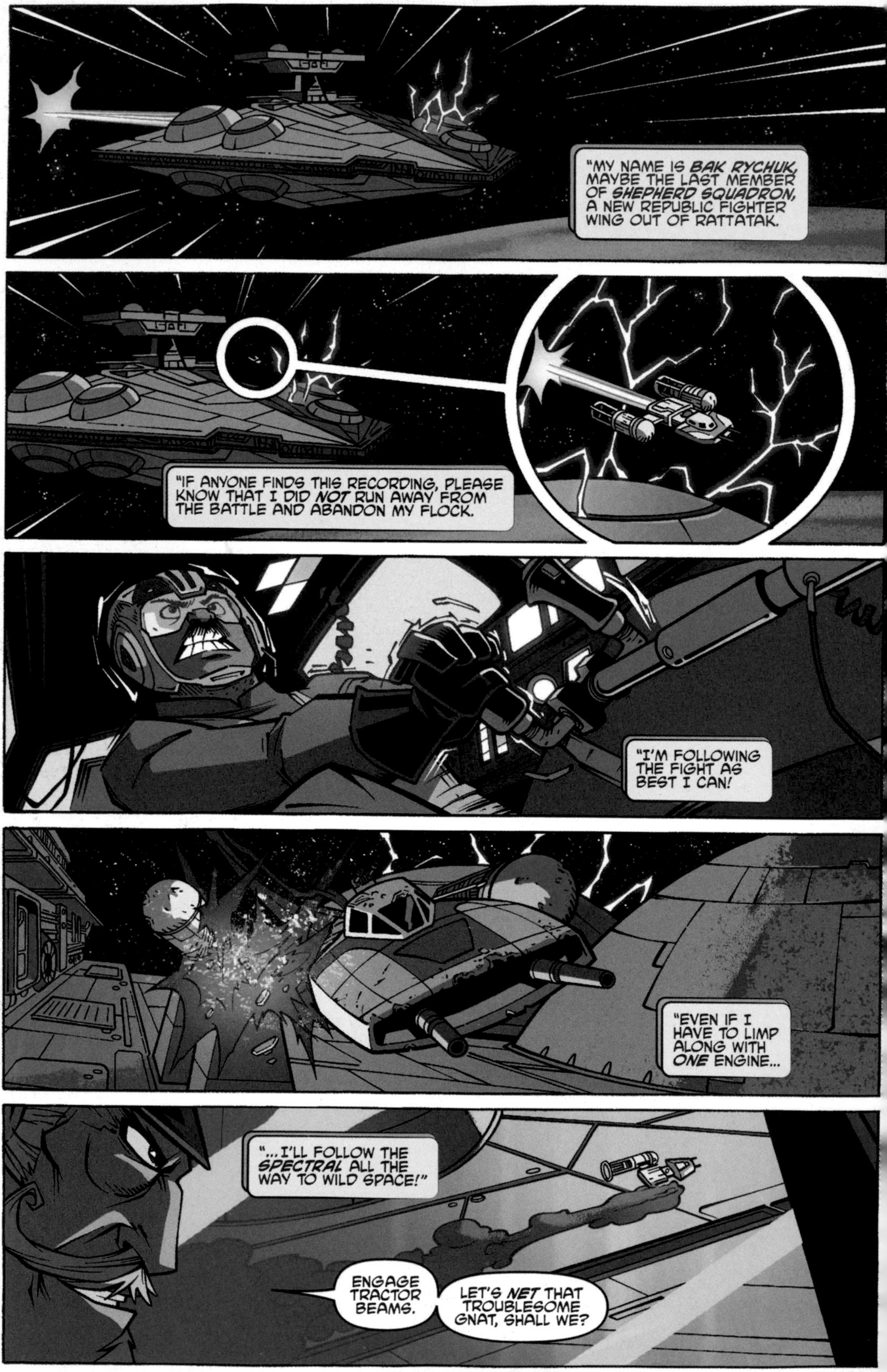
"MY NAME IS BAK RYCHUK, MAYBE THE LAST MEMBER OF SHEPHERD SQUADRON, A NEW REPUBLIC FIGHTER WING OUT OF RATTATAK.
"IF ANYONE FINDS THIS RECORDING, PLEASE KNOW THAT I DID NOT RUN AWAY FROM THE BATTLE AND ABANDON MY FLOCK.
"I'M FOLLOWING THE FIGHT AS BEST I CAN!
"EVEN IF I HAVE TO LIMP ALONG WITH ONE ENGINE...
"...I'LL FOLLOW THE SPECTRAL ALL THE WAY TO WILD SPACE!"
ENGAGE TRACTOR BEAMS.
LET'S NET THAT TROUBLESOME GNAT, SHALL WE?

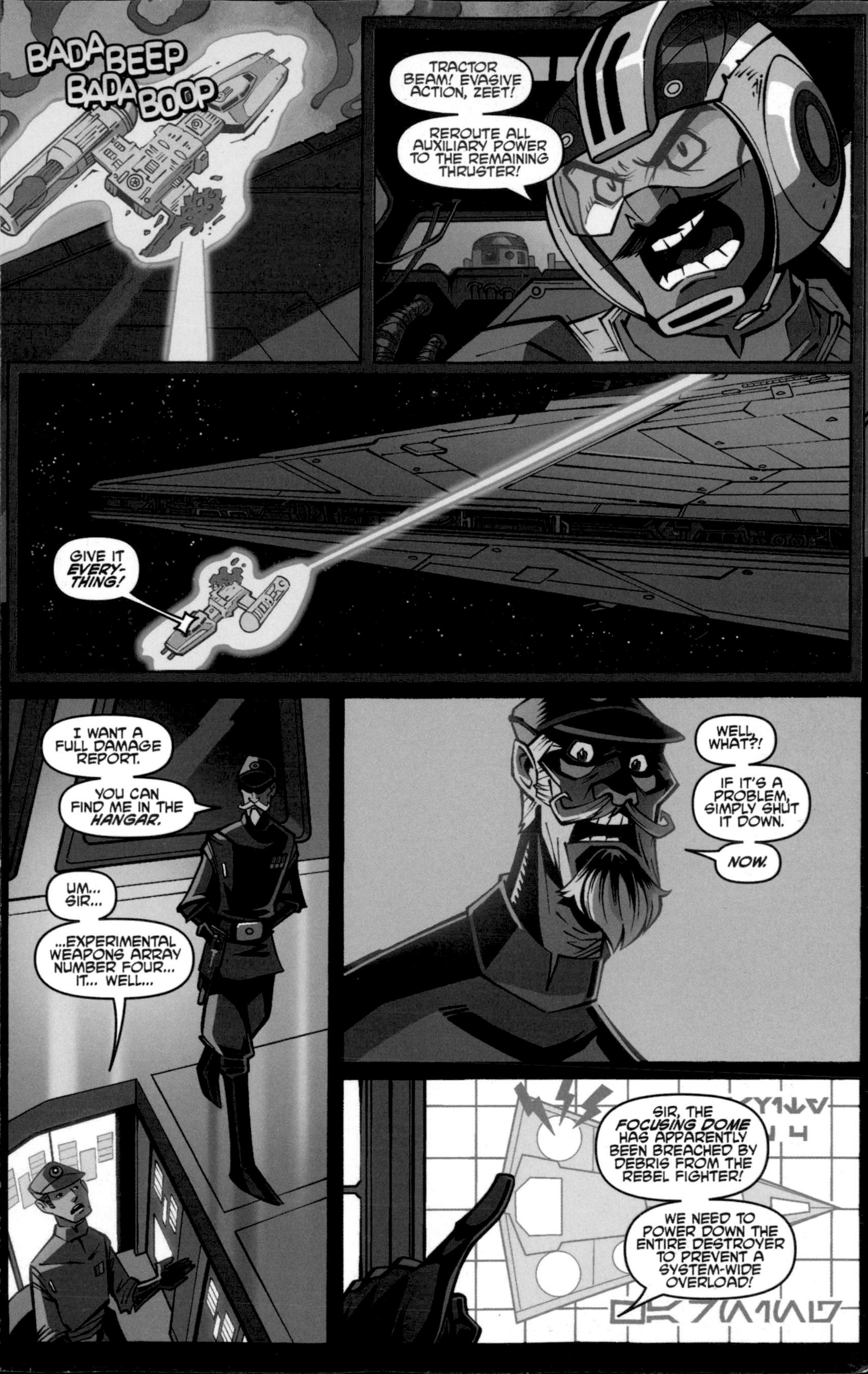
BADA BEEP BADA BOOP
TRACTOR BEAM! EVASIVE ACTION, ZEET!
REROUTE ALL AUXILIARY POWER TO THE REMAINING THRUSTER!
GIVE IT EVERY-THING!
I WANT A FULL DAMAGE REPORT.
YOU CAN FIND ME IN THE HANGAR.
UM... SIR...
...EXPERIMENTAL WEAPONS ARRAY NUMBER FOUR... IT... WELL...
WELL, WHAT?!
IF IT'S A PROBLEM, SIMPLY SHUT IT DOWN.
NOW.
SIR, THE FOCUSING DOME HAS APPARENTLY BEEN BREACHED BY DEBRIS FROM THE REBEL FIGHTER!
WE NEED TO POWER DOWN THE ENTIRE DESTROYER TO PREVENT A SYSTEM-WIDE OVERLOAD!

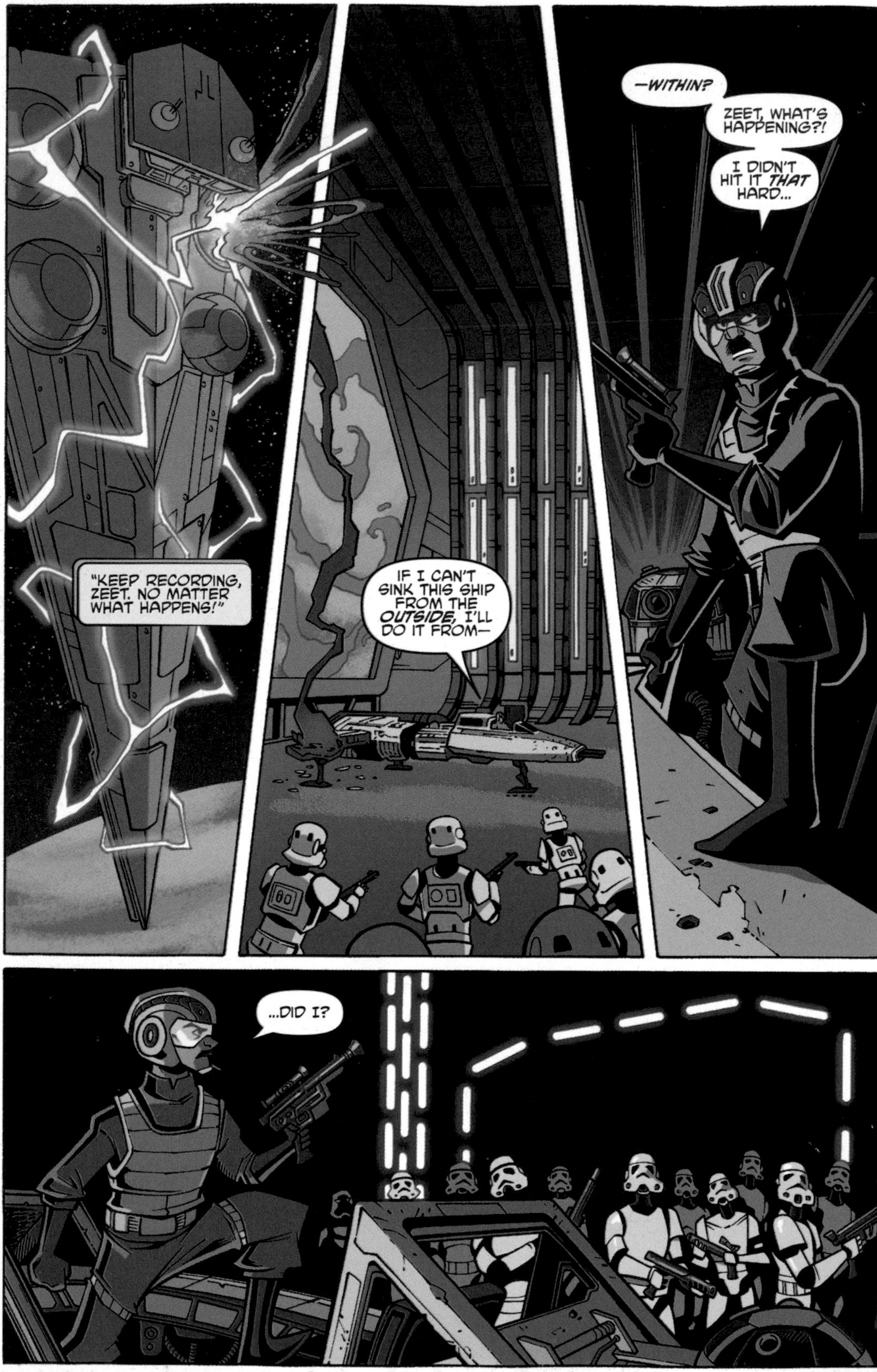
"KEEP RECORDING, ZEET. NO MATTER WHAT HAPPENS!"
IF I CAN'T SINK THIS SHIP FROM THE *OUTSIDE,* I'LL DO IT FROM—
—*WITHIN?*
ZEET, WHAT'S HAPPENING?!
I DIDN'T HIT IT *THAT* HARD...
...DID I?

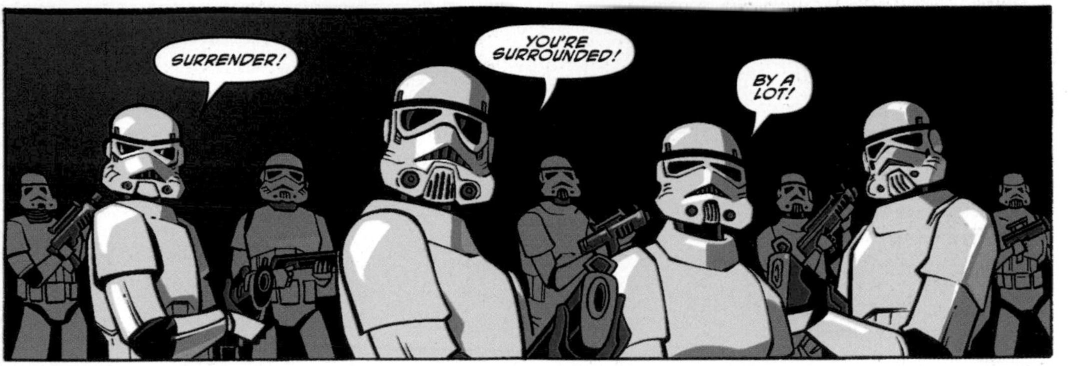
SURRENDER!
YOU'RE SURROUNDED!
BY A LOT!

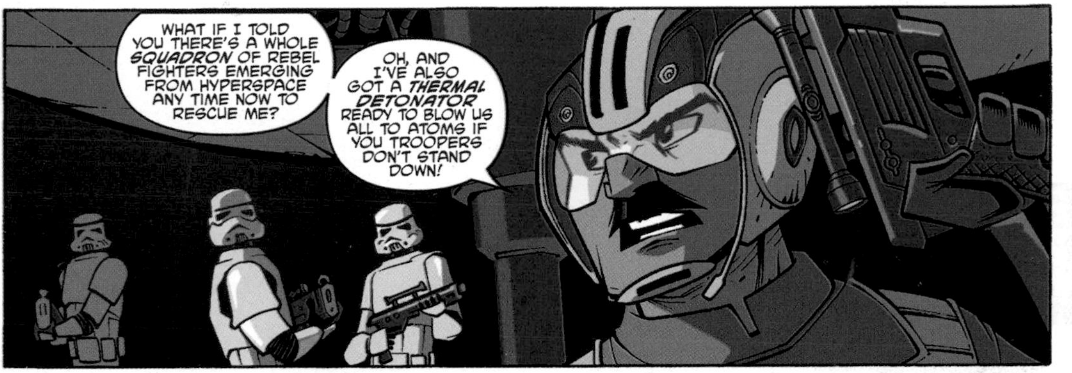
WHAT IF I TOLD YOU THERE'S A WHOLE SQUADRON OF REBEL FIGHTERS EMERGING FROM HYPERSPACE ANY TIME NOW TO RESCUE ME?
OH, AND I'VE ALSO GOT A THERMAL DETONATOR READY TO BLOW US ALL TO ATOMS IF YOU TROOPERS DON'T STAND DOWN!

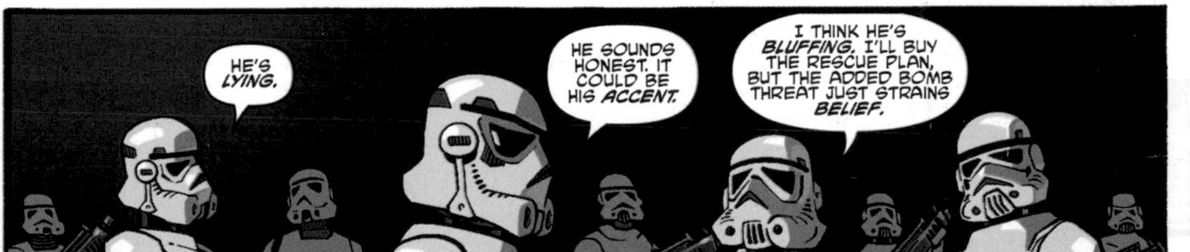
HE'S LYING.
HE SOUNDS HONEST. IT COULD BE HIS ACCENT.
I THINK HE'S BLUFFING. I'LL BUY THE RESCUE PLAN, BUT THE ADDED BOMB THREAT JUST STRAINS BELIEF.

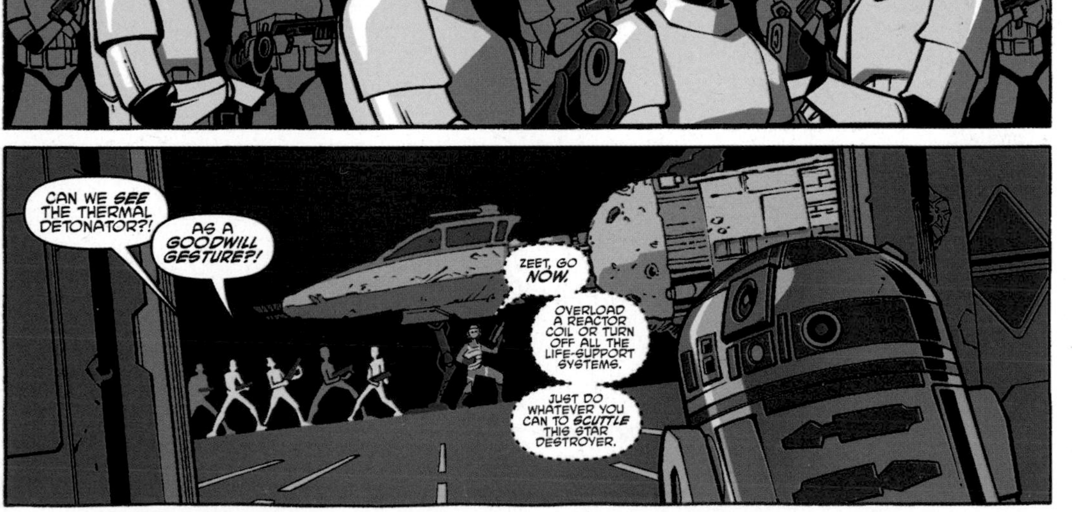
CAN WE SEE THE THERMAL DETONATOR?!
AS A GOODWILL GESTURE?!
ZEET, GO NOW.
OVERLOAD A REACTOR COIL OR TURN OFF ALL THE LIFE-SUPPORT SYSTEMS.
JUST DO WHATEVER YOU CAN TO SCUTTLE THIS STAR DESTROYER.

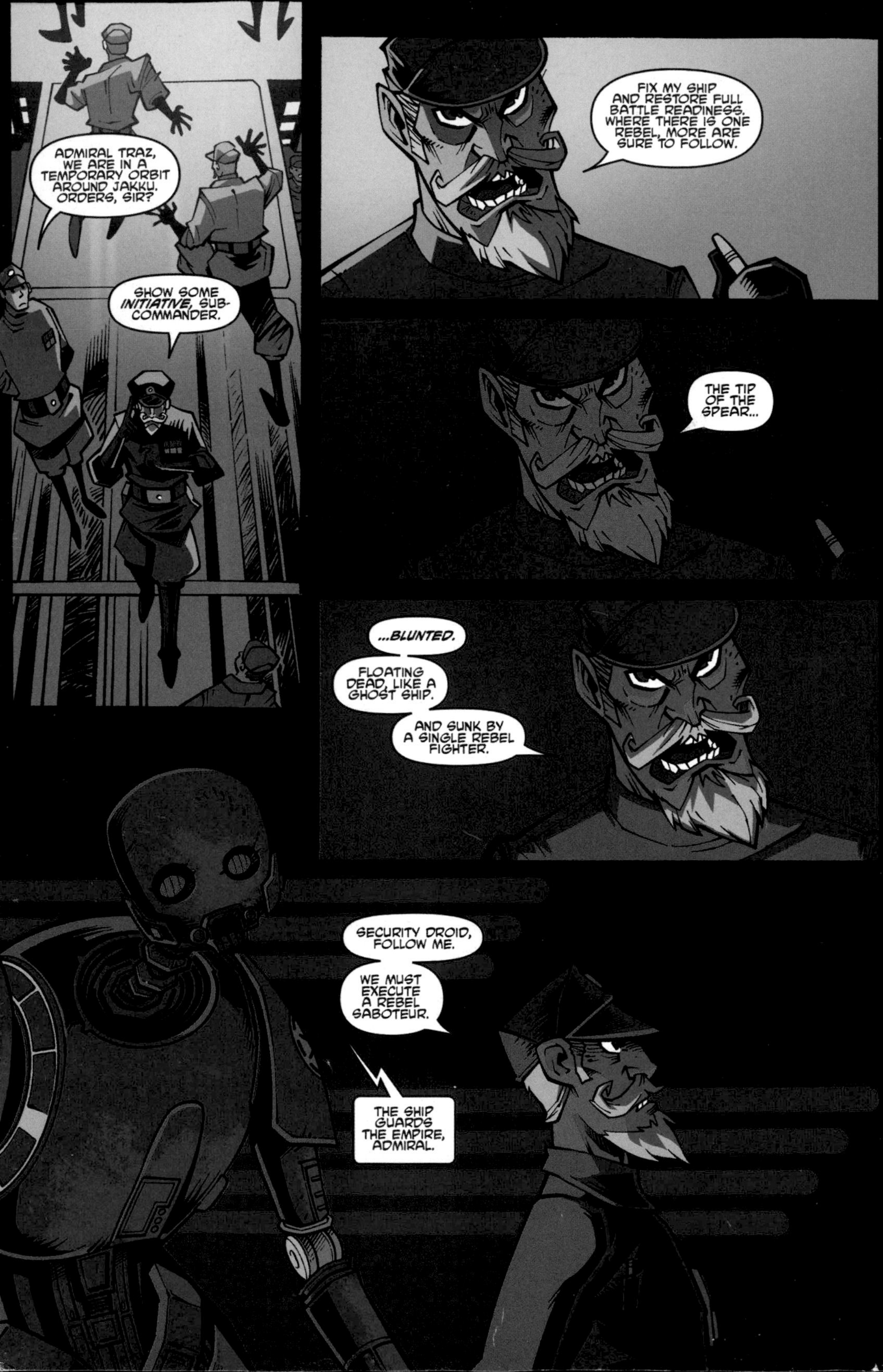
ADMIRAL TRAZ, WE ARE IN A TEMPORARY ORBIT AROUND JAKKU. ORDERS, SIR?
SHOW SOME *INITIATIVE*, SUB-COMMANDER.
FIX MY SHIP AND RESTORE FULL BATTLE READINESS. WHERE THERE IS ONE REBEL, MORE ARE SURE TO FOLLOW.
THE TIP OF THE SPEAR...
...*BLUNTED.*
FLOATING DEAD, LIKE A GHOST SHIP.
AND SUNK BY A SINGLE REBEL FIGHTER.
SECURITY DROID, FOLLOW ME.
WE MUST EXECUTE A REBEL SABOTEUR.
THE SHIP GUARDS THE EMPIRE, ADMIRAL.

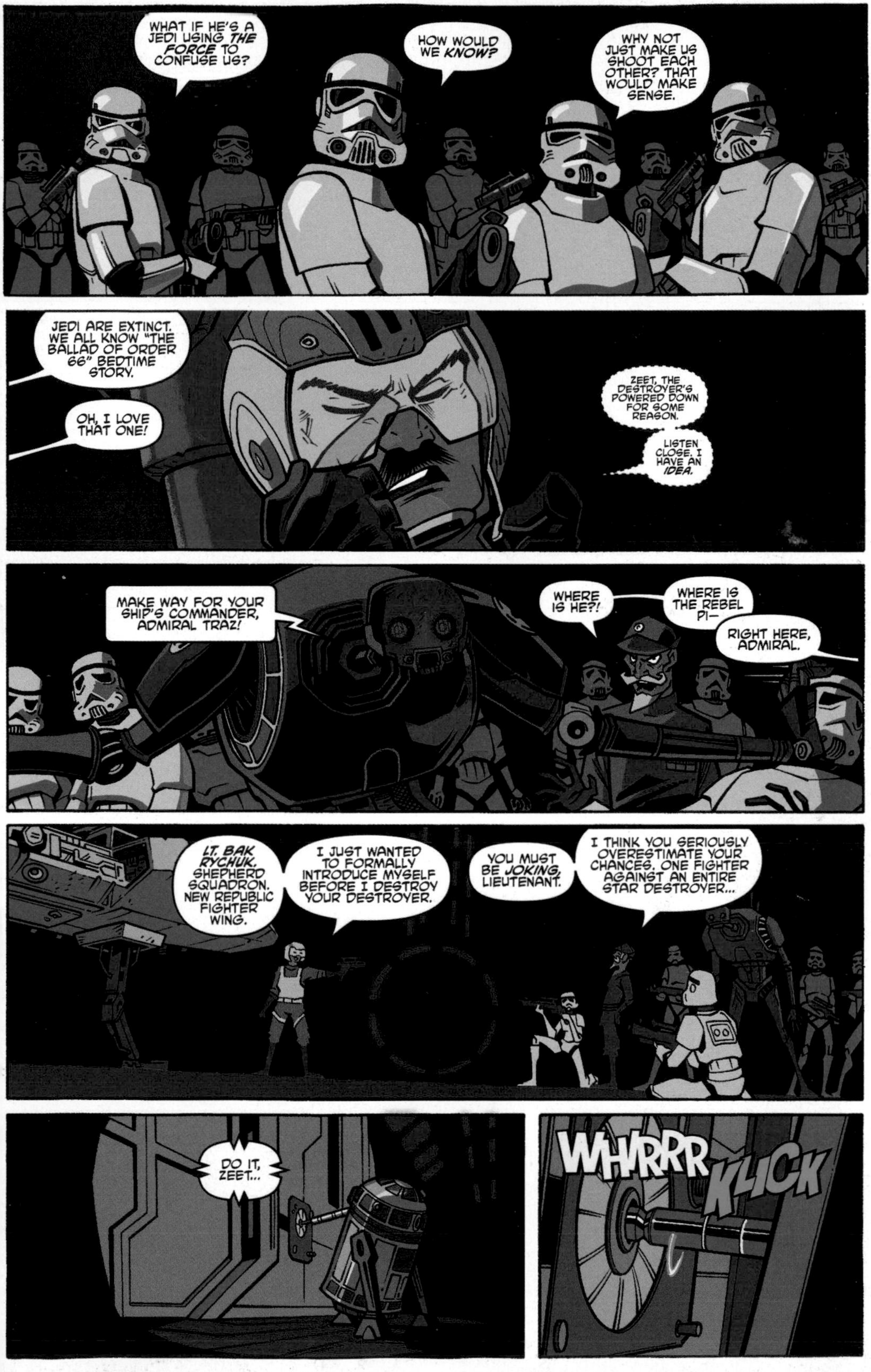
WHAT IF HE'S A JEDI USING THE FORCE TO CONFUSE US?
HOW WOULD WE KNOW?
WHY NOT JUST MAKE US SHOOT EACH OTHER? THAT WOULD MAKE SENSE.
JEDI ARE EXTINCT. WE ALL KNOW "THE BALLAD OF ORDER 66" BEDTIME STORY.
OH, I LOVE THAT ONE!
ZEET, THE DESTROYER'S POWERED DOWN FOR SOME REASON.
LISTEN CLOSE. I HAVE AN IDEA.
MAKE WAY FOR YOUR SHIP'S COMMANDER, ADMIRAL TRAZ!
WHERE IS HE?!
WHERE IS THE REBEL PI—
RIGHT HERE, ADMIRAL.
LT. BAK RYCHUK. SHEPHERD SQUADRON. NEW REPUBLIC FIGHTER WING.
I JUST WANTED TO FORMALLY INTRODUCE MYSELF BEFORE I DESTROY YOUR DESTROYER.
YOU MUST BE JOKING, LIEUTENANT.
I THINK YOU SERIOUSLY OVERESTIMATE YOUR CHANCES. ONE FIGHTER AGAINST AN ENTIRE STAR DESTROYER...
DO IT, ZEET...
WHIRRR
KLICK

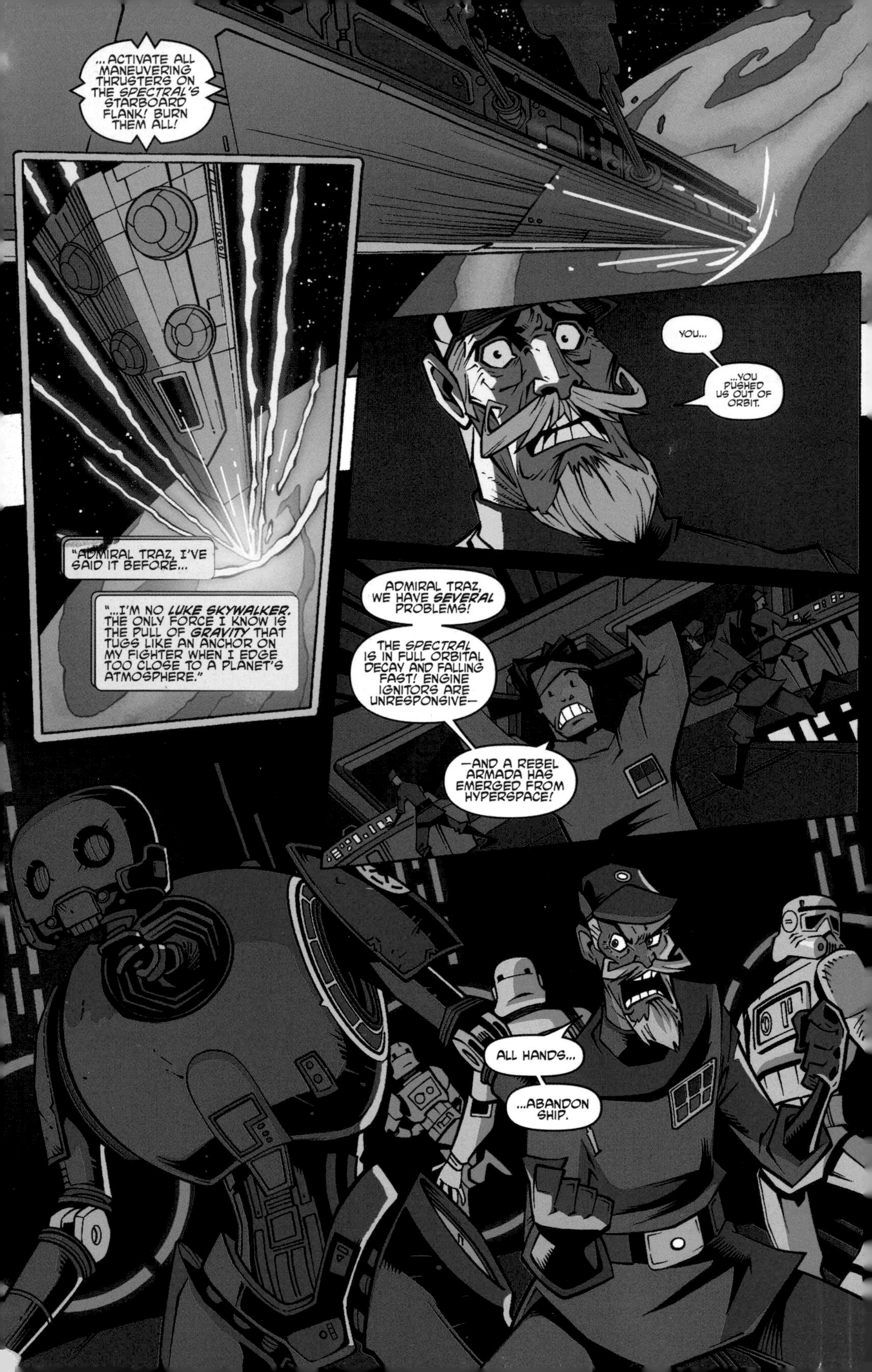
...ACTIVATE ALL MANEUVERING THRUSTERS ON THE SPECTRAL'S STARBOARD FLANK! BURN THEM ALL!
"ADMIRAL TRAZ, I'VE SAID IT BEFORE...
"...I'M NO LUKE SKYWALKER. THE ONLY FORCE I KNOW IS THE PULL OF GRAVITY THAT TUGS LIKE AN ANCHOR ON MY FIGHTER WHEN I EDGE TOO CLOSE TO A PLANET'S ATMOSPHERE."
YOU...
...YOU PUSHED US OUT OF ORBIT.
ADMIRAL TRAZ, WE HAVE SEVERAL PROBLEMS!
THE SPECTRAL IS IN FULL ORBITAL DECAY AND FALLING FAST! ENGINE IGNITORS ARE UNRESPONSIVE—
—AND A REBEL ARMADA HAS EMERGED FROM HYPERSPACE!
ALL HANDS...
...ABANDON SHIP.

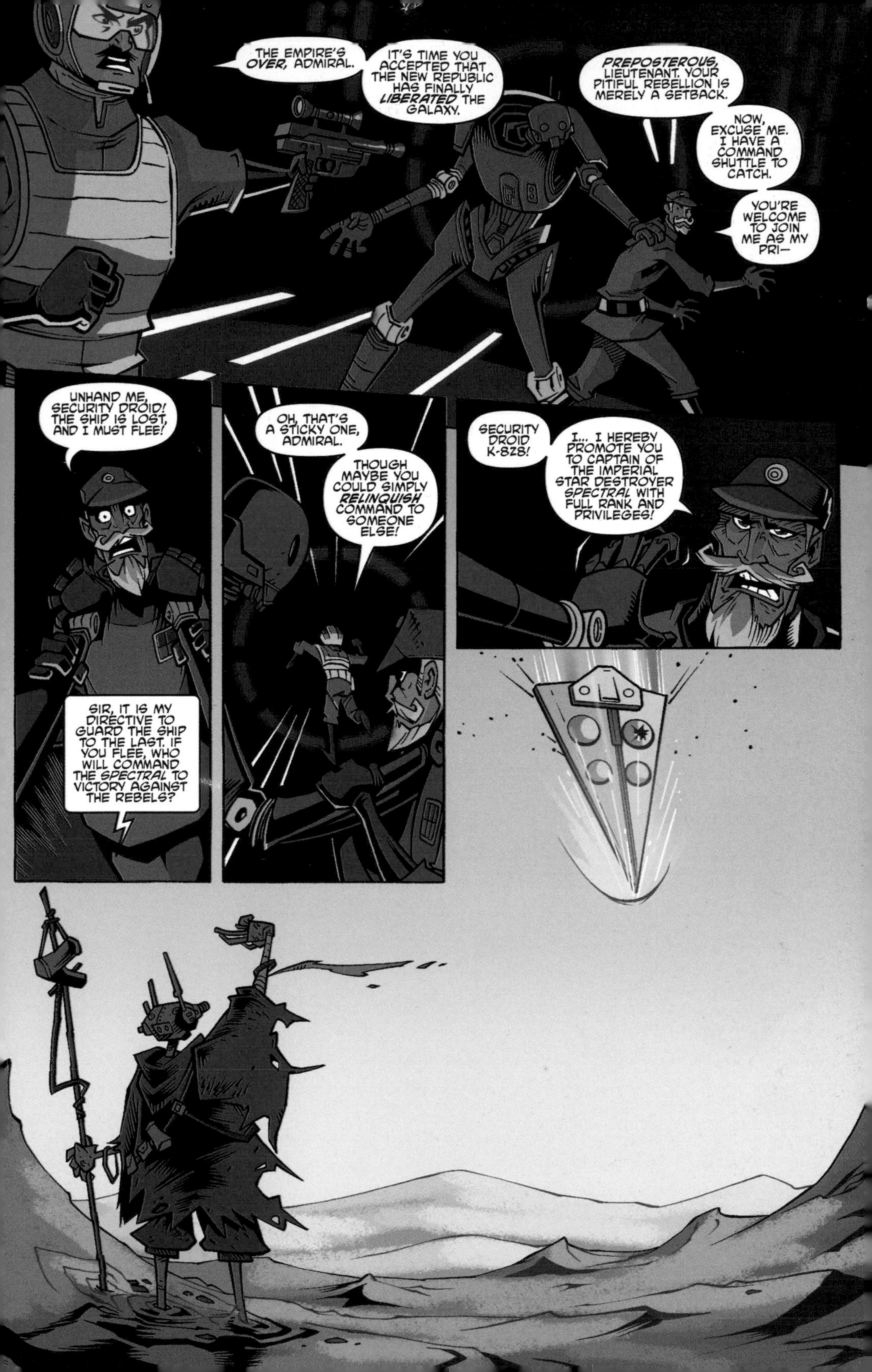
THE EMPIRE'S OVER, ADMIRAL.
IT'S TIME YOU ACCEPTED THAT THE NEW REPUBLIC HAS FINALLY LIBERATED THE GALAXY.
PREPOSTEROUS, LIEUTENANT. YOUR PITIFUL REBELLION IS MERELY A SETBACK.
NOW, EXCUSE ME. I HAVE A COMMAND SHUTTLE TO CATCH.
YOU'RE WELCOME TO JOIN ME AS MY PRI—
UNHAND ME, SECURITY DROID! THE SHIP IS LOST, AND I MUST FLEE!
SIR, IT IS MY DIRECTIVE TO GUARD THE SHIP TO THE LAST. IF YOU FLEE, WHO WILL COMMAND THE SPECTRAL TO VICTORY AGAINST THE REBELS?
OH, THAT'S A STICKY ONE, ADMIRAL.
THOUGH MAYBE YOU COULD SIMPLY RELINQUISH COMMAND TO SOMEONE ELSE!
SECURITY DROID K-8Z8!
I... I HEREBY PROMOTE YOU TO CAPTAIN OF THE IMPERIAL STAR DESTROYER SPECTRAL WITH FULL RANK AND PRIVILEGES!

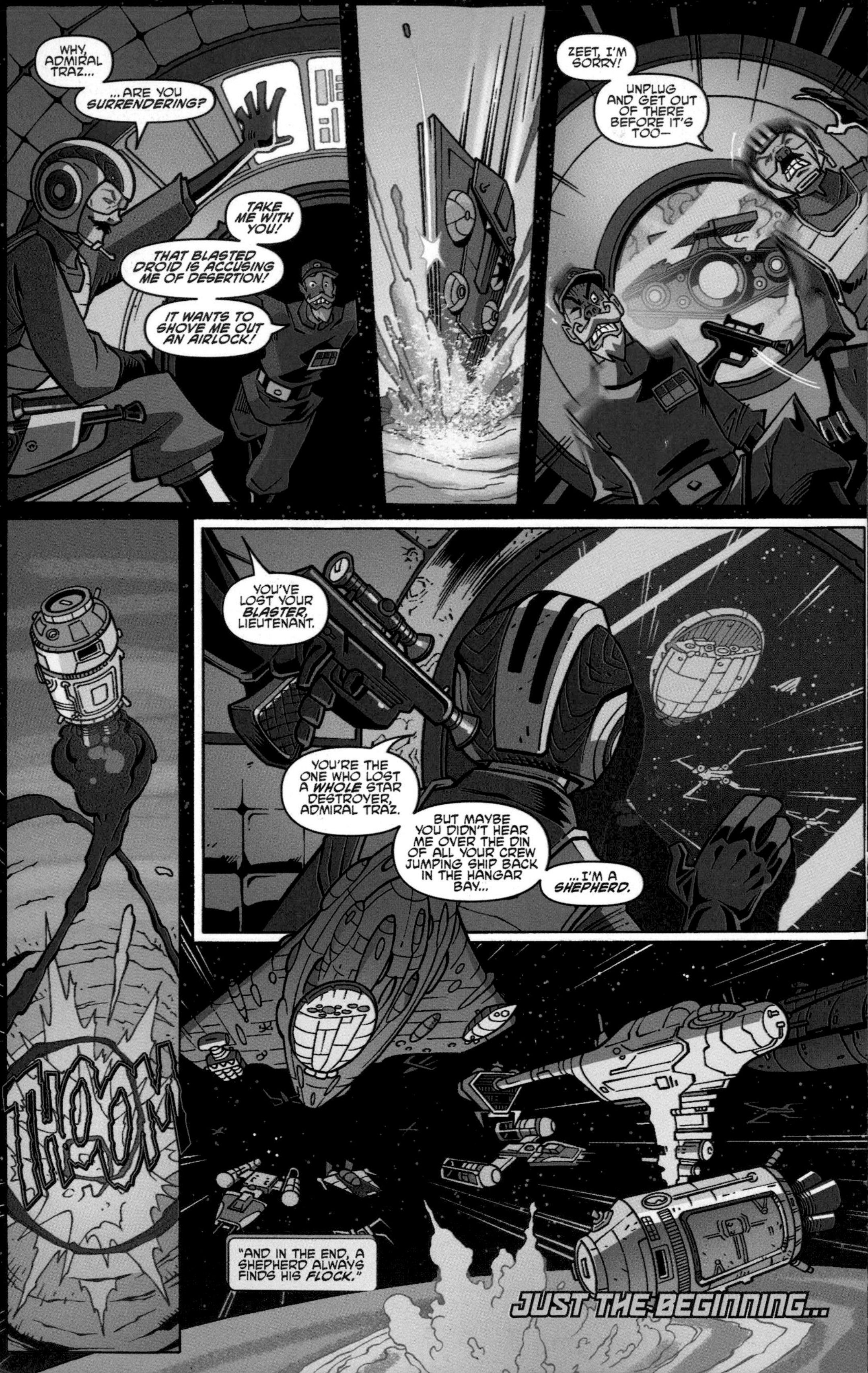
WHY, ADMIRAL TRAZ...
...ARE YOU *SURRENDERING?*
TAKE ME WITH YOU!
THAT BLASTED DROID IS ACCUSING ME OF DESERTION!
IT WANTS TO SHOVE ME OUT AN AIRLOCK!
ZEET, I'M SORRY!
UNPLUG AND GET OUT OF THERE BEFORE IT'S TOO—
YOU'VE LOST YOUR *BLASTER,* LIEUTENANT.
YOU'RE THE ONE WHO LOST A *WHOLE* STAR DESTROYER, ADMIRAL TRAZ.
BUT MAYBE YOU DIDN'T HEAR ME OVER THE DIN OF ALL YOUR CREW JUMPING SHIP BACK IN THE HANGAR BAY...
...I'M A *SHEPHERD.*
THOOM
"AND IN THE END, A SHEPHERD ALWAYS FINDS HIS *FLOCK.*"
JUST THE BEGINNING...

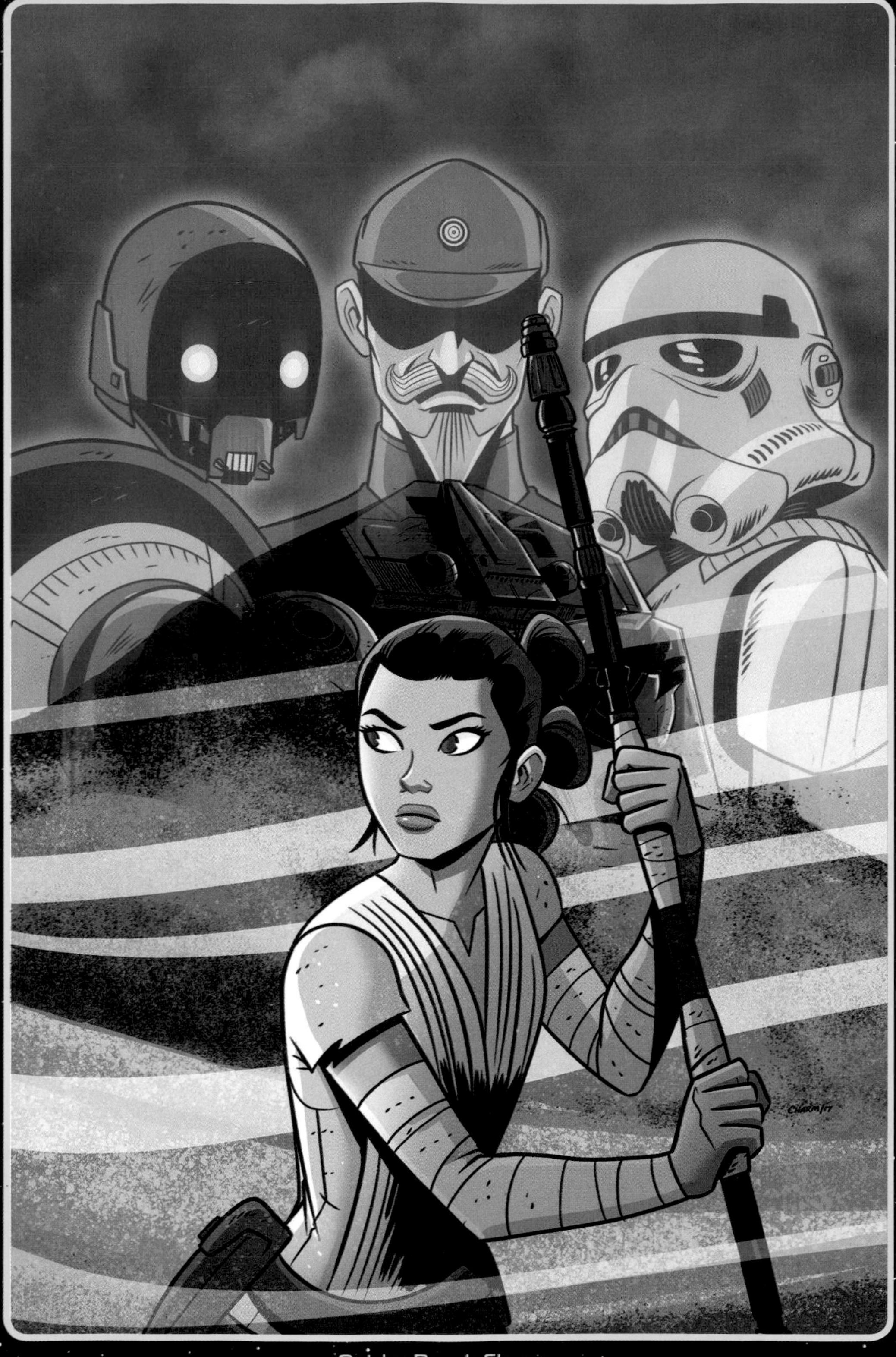
CHARM/17

Art by Derek Charm

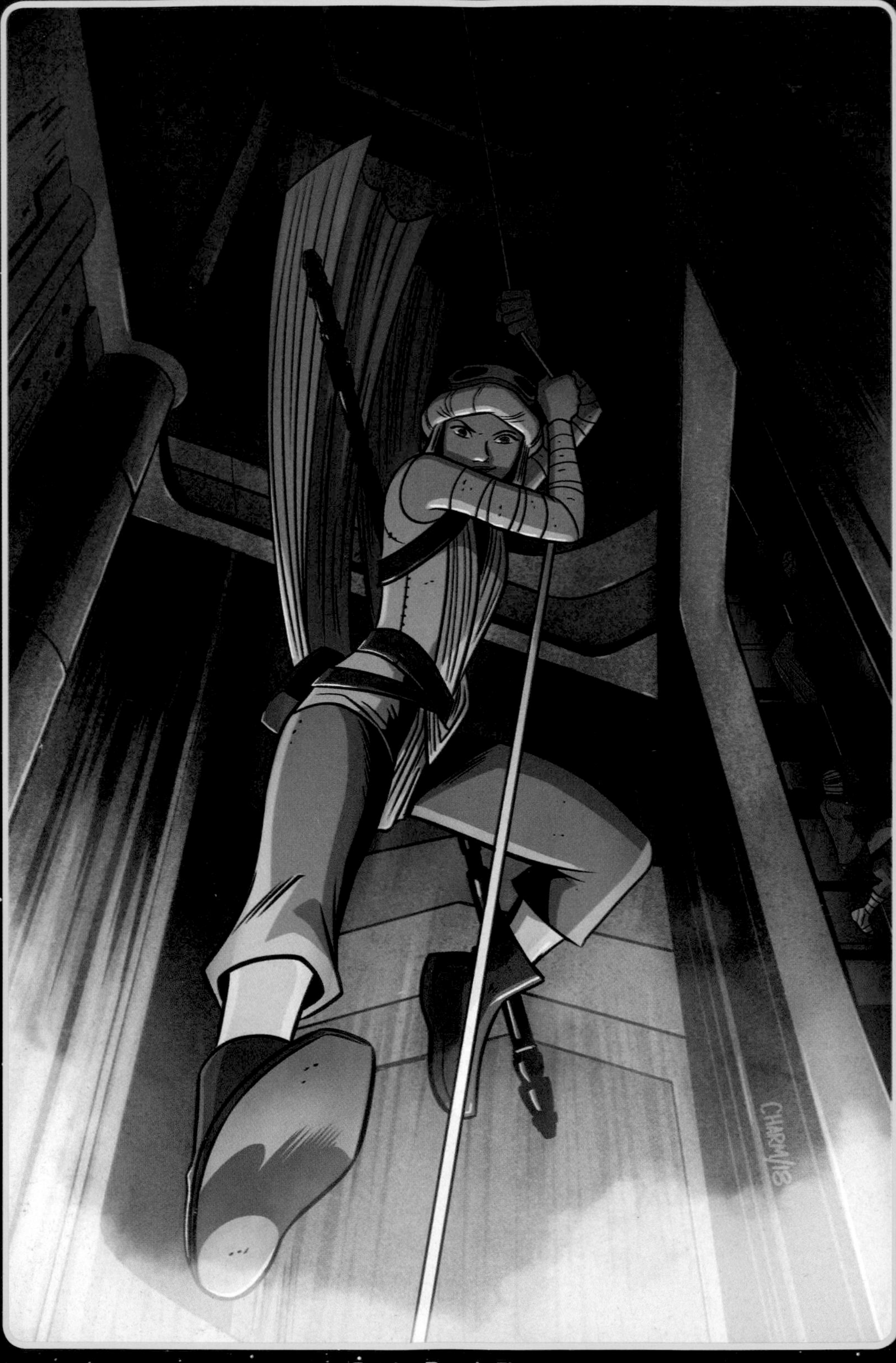
CHARM/18

Art by Derek Charm

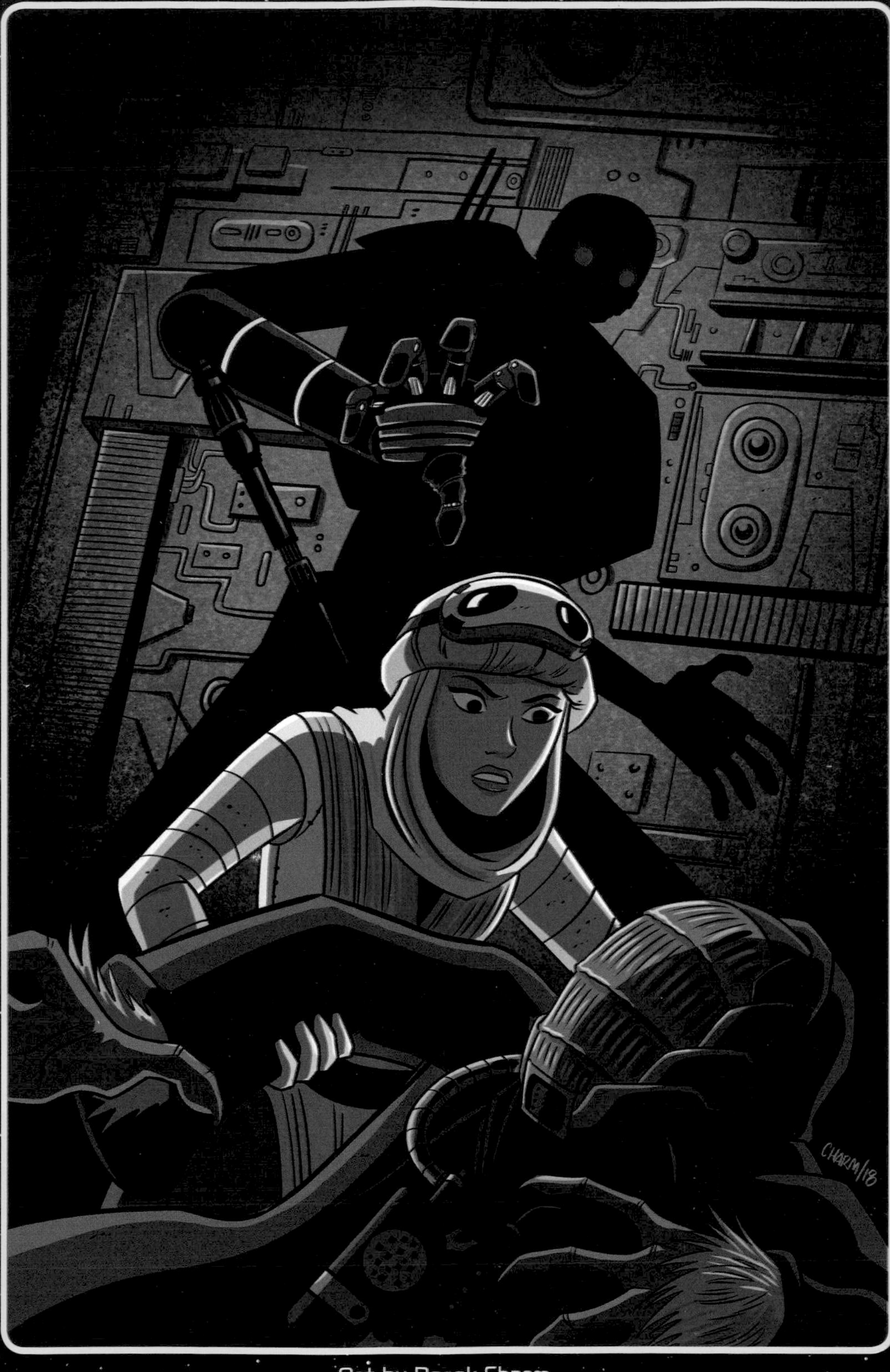
CHARM/18

Art by Derek Charm

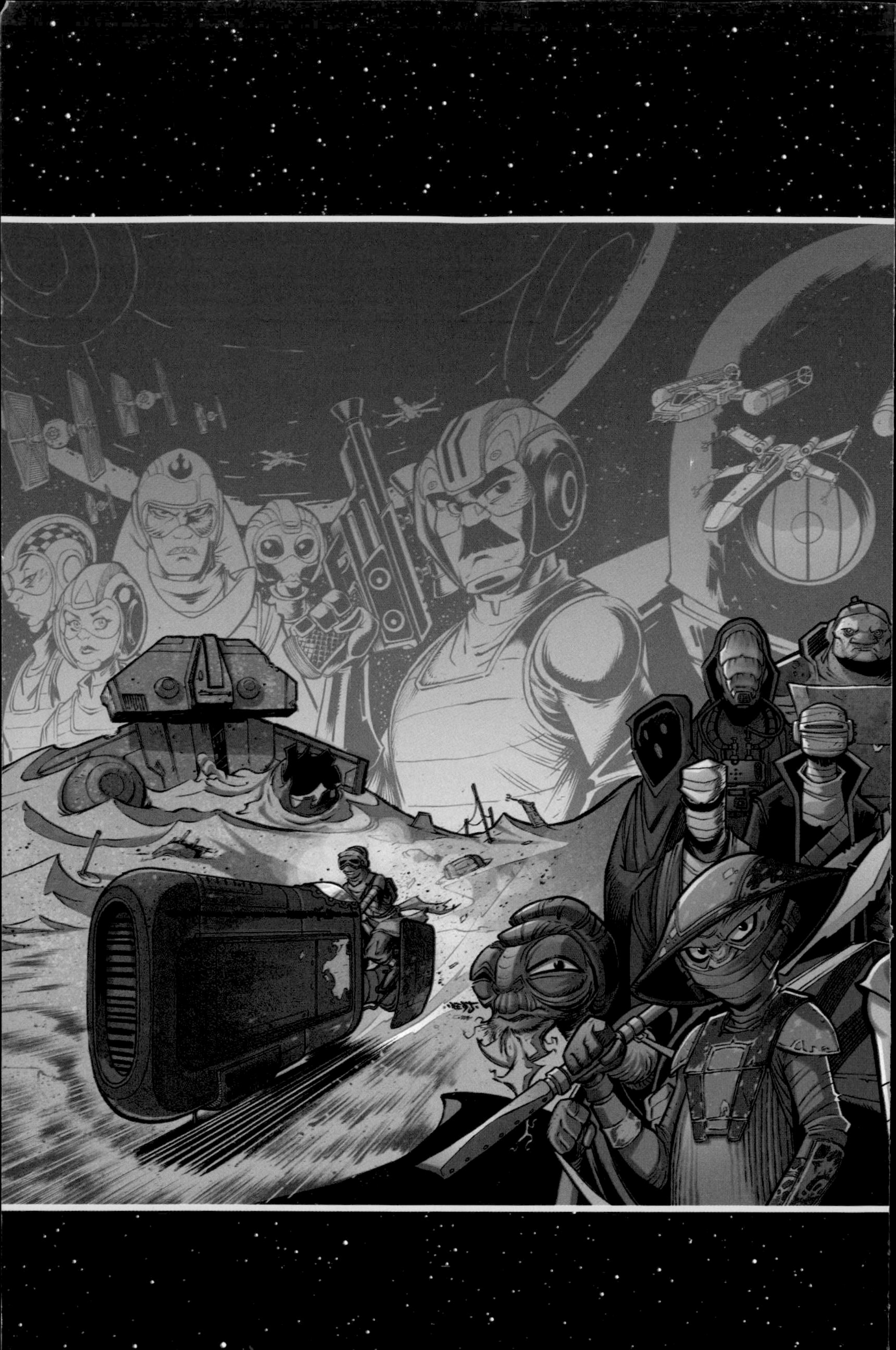

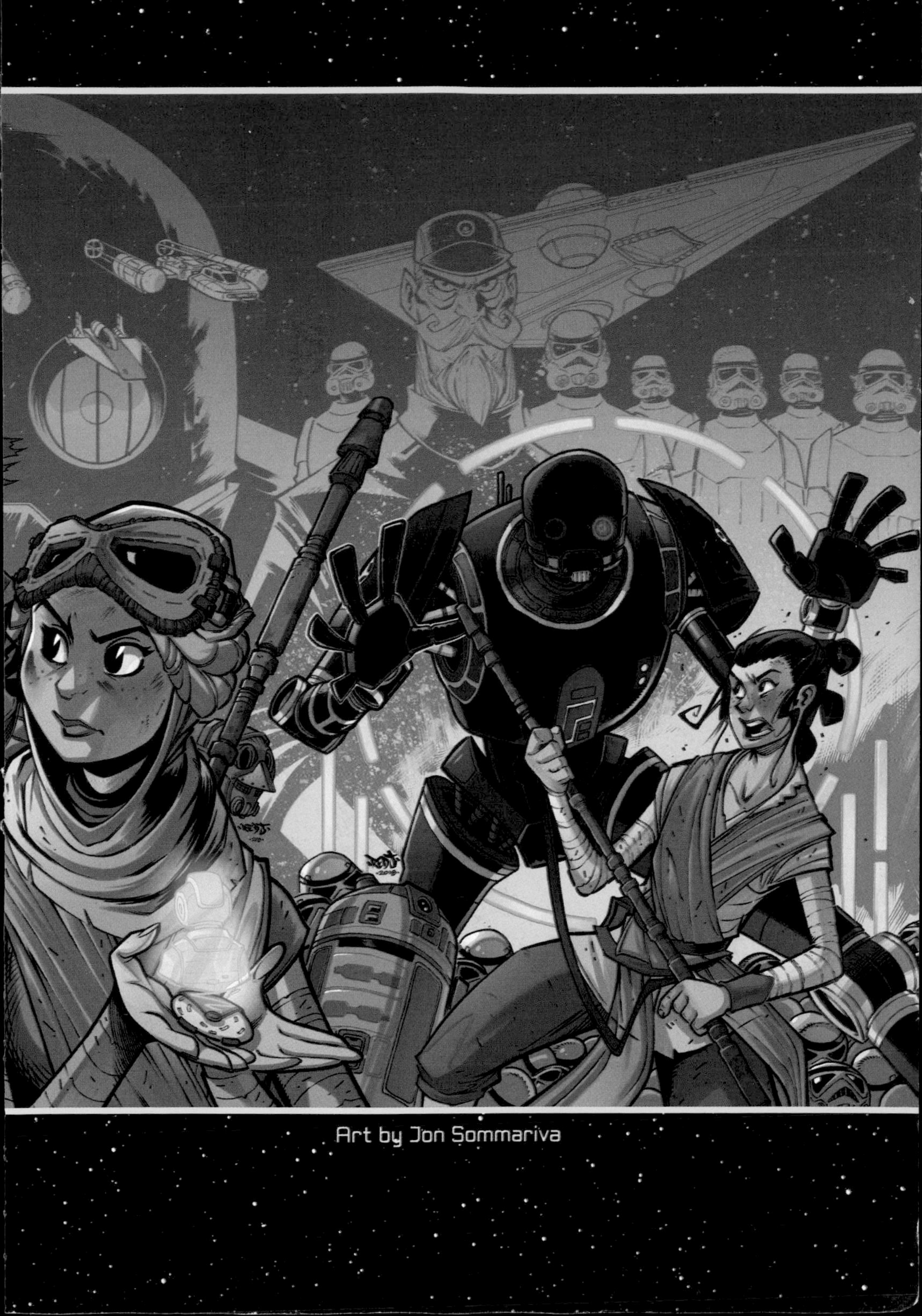

Art by Jon Sommariva